CORNELIUS' REVENGE

(Otherwise known as *Revenge of Cornelius*)

Book Two of The Cornelius Saga Series

Tanya R. Taylor

TABLE OF CONTENTS

Books Currently in This Series

Book One: *Cornelius*
Book Two: *Cornelius' Revenge*
Book Three: *CARA*
Book Four: *We See No Evil*
Book Five: *The Contract: Murder in*
The Bahamas
Book Six: *The Lost Children of Atlantis*
Book Seven: *Death of an Angel*
Book Eight: *The Groundskeeper*
Book Nine: CARA: *The Beginning—MATILDA'S STORY*
Book Ten: *The Disappearing House*
Book Eleven: *Wicked Little Saints*

Don't miss out on new book releases. Join Tanya's
Mailing List at: www.tanya-R-taylor.com

First book in this best-selling series.

"Hauntingly beautiful…"

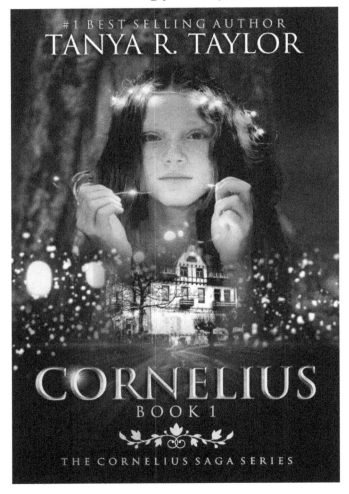

To all my readers,
Thank You.

1

"Rosie, hurry up! We can't miss our flight," Mira yelled while tying her shoe laces.

"I'm ready now, Mom." Six-year-old Rosie Cullen entered the bedroom moments later. Her pink and white back-pack hung sturdily across a pink, short-sleeved blouse with frilly sleeves. Blue jeans slackly covered her legs and matching, pink tennis shoes snuggled her tiny feet. Her black, medium-length candy curls glistened from the extra spiff of her mother's oil sheen. "See, Mom, we look just alike now, except for your blouse— it's blue. I told you pink is fancier."

8

Mira smiled. "You're probably right, Rosie, but Mom didn't have any pink blouse like yours. Sorry." She stood up. "All set?"

"All set!"

"Perfect! Let's go, then." Mira grabbed the two carry-ons as Rosie led the way to the front door.

Abruptly, the little girl stopped and looked back at her mother. "Is Uncle Wade coming too?"

"I'm afraid not, honey."

"Well, who will I play with at Nana and Pops' house? I'll be so bored. Why can't Uncle Wade send Tommy?" She sulked.

Mira crouched down to her daughter's level. "Your Uncle Wade and Aunt Norma are very busy at the hospital right now. They couldn't break away to fly up the same time as we are and they won't send Tommy on the plane alone."

"So when will we ever see them again? I miss them!" Rosie's big, brown eyes had a tinge of sadness in them.

"I'm sure we'll see them soon. Maybe we'll take a trip down there to The Bahamas one weekend or they can come here to L.A. How'd you like that?" Mira hoped the proposition would excite the child.

"That sounds neat, Mom!" Rosie's mood suddenly elevated. "Okay, let's go." She opened the door and headed outside toward the waiting cab.

Passing the champagne-colored Mitsubishi parked in the driveway in front of their white condominium, Rosie asked: "Why can't we take our own car to the airport, Mom?"

"Because I don't want to have to yank my hair out from the hefty fee I'd have to pay when we get back, honey."

"Good morning, Ma'am." The driver was standing next to the cab. He was of slim build; had a prickly beard and dirty-blonde hair tied into a ponytail. Looked like he was well into his fifties.

"Good morning." Mira smiled back, then looked at Rosie.

"Good morning, sir," she said.

"I'll get that for you." The driver quickly opened the back door and Rosie climbed inside.

"Thanks for coming," Mira said to him.

"My pleasure." He took the luggage and placed them in the trunk.

Mira slid inside next to Rosie as the little girl prissily positioned herself onto the leather seat.

"You look beautiful, Mom."

"And so do you, my little princess." Mira tucked back the child's hair.

The cab driver got in and started the engine. He cleared his throat and glanced back at Mira through the rear-view mirror. "All set?" He asked.

Mira's eyes met his. "Yes, we are."

They were on their way.

* * *

"Mom, can I sit by the window?" Rosie asked excitedly.

"Excuse me," a young man said as he brushed past Mira and Rosie who had just arrived at their appointed row.

"Sure honey, you can sit at the window," Mira answered.

11

Rosie quickly went through and climbed onto the seat. After resting her backpack on top of her lap, she buckled her own seat belt, then eagerly peered out of the window.

"Those men look like ants down there," she remarked.

"No, they don't!" Mira laughed as she fastened her seat-belt. "We haven't lifted off yet. How can they look like ants from this short distance?"

"Well, they do to me!" Rosie returned.

"My goodness… what beautiful hair you have, little girl!" An elderly lady commented as she was slowly passing by.

"Thank you, Ma'am!" Rosie shifted proudly in her seat, pressing her lips together as if she were the queen of that flying castle.

"She seems rather classy too." The lady bent down slightly toward Mira; voice lowered.

"She does. Doesn't she?" Mira grinned.

Smiling, the nice stranger continued on to one of the back rows.

"Can I put that into the overhead compartment for you?" a beautifully-attired attendant asked. She was referring to Rosie's backpack.

"Does she have to take it, Mom?" Rosie pouted.

"You can put it under your seat instead. Would you prefer that?" The lady offered.

"Yes, Ma'am."

"I'll take it for you," Mira reached over and placed it under Rosie's seat as the flight attendant walked off.

Everyone sat quietly as the plane revved for the take-off.

"Ready?" Mira asked Rosie who was looking out the window again. By then, the tarmac was clear.

"Yes, I'm ready. I'm ready to see Nana and Pops again. Are you ready?"

Mira could not recall Rosie's smile being any cuter.

"Yes. We're going to have a great time there. Mom and Dad are so excited to see you again."

"I'm excited to see them too!"

As the plane took off and smoothly elevated into the clear, blue sky, Mira looked over at the ground below.

"Everything down there looks like ants now, don't it?" Rosie turned to her mother.

"Yes, honey."

After a few moments, Mira rested her head on the head-rest. As she shut her eyes, her life in recent years suddenly flashed before her. Before long, she successfully blocked it all out and drifted off into a dreamless sleep.

2

"Mom! Wake up!" Rosie shook her.

Mira peeled open her eyes, looked at Rosie, then around at other passengers who were getting ready to leave the plane. "We're here already?" she asked weakly.

"Mom, you slept the whole while!" Rosie's hand was at her side.

"I...I'm sorry, honey." She raised her eyebrows.

The cabin door opened and persons were filing out of the aircraft. She glanced Rosie's way and realized she already had her backpack on her lap. They both waited until most of the passengers had exited the plane before getting up to join what was left of the line.

"I can't believe we're here already," Mira said quietly as the little girl stood in front of her.

"Time flies. Doesn't it, Mom?"

"It surely does."

With luggage in hand, they followed the others through the long corridor with all its twists and turns, then headed toward the exit. It was a beautiful day in Mizpah and they were so glad to have arrived.

"There's Nana and Pops!" Rosie pointed to her waving grandparents who were standing several feet away from the exit. She took off running toward them and Michael knelt down happily awaiting her. She flew into his arms as Sara hugged her from behind.

It had been several months since Mira last saw her father, but it was obvious that within that time-frame, he had lost a considerable amount of weight. *Must be all that yard work*, she thought.

"So what am I...chopped liver?" she asked, approaching them.

"Oh, honey, I'm so glad you two are here, safe and sound!" Sara embraced her.

Michael stood and hugged Mira as well.

"How are you doing?" he asked.

"Just great, Dad. How are you?"

"Swell! Let me take those." He was referring to the luggage.

Mira released one of the bags and held on to the other. She didn't want him doing much lifting since he had been recently having occasional back pains.

He grabbed the other one as well.

"Dad, I could've managed that," Mira said.

"I'm sure you could, but I can too." He carried them over to the trunk.

"I'm so glad you two are here!" Sara pressed her face against her daughter's.

"We're happy to be here, Mom," Mira replied.

They walked over to the car together.

"How's Dad doing? He seems to have trimmed down quite a bit lately."

"Oh...yes. He's watching his diet more these days. You know him—likes to look his best. I heard from your brother this morning." She changed the subject rather abruptly.

"Oh? What's he saying?"

"He was just wondering if you and Rosie had arrived yet and said he wished he could have come, but he's so tied up at work right now."

"I know. We spoke last night. Rosie really wished Tommy would've been here." She spoke quietly as the little girl stood proudly beside her grandfather at the car filling him in on all the details of their flight.

"Yes, they're so close," Sara returned.

"She'll be fine, though. I'll find things to do to keep her busy during the two weeks we're here."

"*You'll* find things?" Sara asked with a smirk. "What're the rest of us… chopped liver?"

They both started laughing as they got into the car.

* * *

"Here we are…" Sara unlocked the kitchen door and allowed Mira and Rosie to enter first. The family always used that entrance since the carport was right adjacent to it. The front door mostly opened whenever guests showed up.

"It's been several months well; hasn't it?" Sara surmised.

"Yeah." Mira sighed.

"Well, I'm glad you sent Rosie ahead last Christmas since you couldn't make it."

Mira sat down in the living room and Rosie climbed up on the couch next to her.

"She had so much fun with Tommy that visit. Didn't you, pumpkin?" Sara smiled at Rosie.

"I sure did, Nana!"

The proud grandmother grinned. "And you'll have just as much fun this time!"

"Will I?" Rosie was excited only for a moment before her intellect kicked in. "But how? Tommy's not here this time."

"Because Nana and Pops are going to give you the time of your little, young life." She sat across from her. "We're going to play lots of games, go to the park, the movie theater…"

"Movies? Really? We're going to see movies?" Rosie's eyes widened.

"Sure. Why not? Anything our little pumpkin wants to do—that's what we're going to do!"

Rosie got up, ran over to her grandmother and hugged her neck tightly. "Oh, Nana... you're the best Nana in the whole world!"

Sara was smiling from ear to ear as Michael passed with the luggage. "These'll be in your room," he said to Mira.

"Thanks, Dad," Mira replied.

"I almost forgot Dad didn't come in," she mumbled softly.

"He's always been as slow as a turtle, you know." Sara laughed.

"Don't say that about Pops!" Rosie exclaimed.

"Sorry, dear. I'm just joking."

A minute later, Michael joined them and sat in his favorite chair—the one with the invisible *Reserved for Michael Cullen* engraved onto the leather.

"So how's everything up there in California?" He asked.

"Everything's fine, Dad."

"The weather's good?"

"Pretty sunny for the most part," Mira indicated.

As she sat with them, Mira reflected on how quickly time had passed. Her parents now had graying hair—though she felt her mother still looked stunning for her age. She was putting in her last couple of years at the hospital after Michael retired from his executive-level position at the Gaming Board.

Mira remembered the years they had spent in that house—many of them held not-so-good memories, but a few did, particularly the ones after Karlen and Andy's saga came to a close. Her father's almost instant transformation into the man they wished he had been ages before was unforgettable and nothing less than remarkable. Despite his limited communication skills which still remained, by all accounts, he became a wonderful and loving husband and father.

"Still work for that chiropractor?" Michael broke the brief silence.

"He's a cardiologist, Dad, and yes, I'm still there," Mira replied.

Sara was looking on. She could tell that her husband had something he wanted to get off his chest, but wasn't so sure if he should."

Mira noticed too. "Rosie, would you like to watch TV in the bedroom for a while?" she asked.

"Sure. Let's go, Pops!" The child turned to her grandfather.

"Honey, how about you and I go?" Sara proposed.

"You and me, Nana?" Rosie appeared somewhat baffled. "But Pops and I always watch TV together. Aren't you coming, Pops?"

Michael managed a smile. "I'll come in a little while, pumpkin."

"Can we watch *The Twilight Zone*?"

"Sure we can, if it's on."

"I'll see if I can find it, okay?"

"Okay, pumpkin," Michael replied.

Sara and Rosie headed to the master bedroom.

Michael cleared his throat. "So, any thoughts on going back to school and getting your degree?" he asked Mira. "You only had... what... a year and a half left? Something like that?"

"I haven't thought about it lately," Mira answered.

"Why not?" The expression on her father's face was one of concern.

"I just haven't, Dad. A lot's been going on lately like work, getting Rosie into school, and a bunch of other things."

"I see."

Mira interlaced her fingers in her lap. "Dad, I know when you and Mom sent me off to college you guys had big dreams for me... and don't get me wrong, I was the one who gave you the idea that I wanted to become a doctor—just like Wade turned out to be. Instead, I got pregnant, dropped out of school and never went back. And on top of that, I know it seems like I settled for working in a doctor's office instead of becoming one like I had intended, so that's probably another 'slap in the face'. I understand where you're coming from, Dad and I'm really sorry I disappointed you and Mom..."

"You didn't disappoint us, Mira," Michael stated, but then noticed the look of disbelief on her face. "Okay, at first your mother and I felt let-down because we did have high hopes for you, but what I need you to know is that we still believe in you and we don't think any less of you because you got pregnant and dropped out of school. We just hate to see you settle for less than what you always wanted to be; that's all."

"Pops!" Rosie emerged with a grimace. "Nana and I can't find *The Twilight Zone*,"

"Okay, pumpkin. I'll be there in a minute," Michael said.

The little girl quickly headed back to the room.

"Dad, I love my job. Doctor Charles is a wonderful employer and I have lots of benefits there at the clinic," Mira explained. "I'm not saying that I won't eventually go back to school and finish what I started. I'm just waiting for the right time and I really don't think it's now."

"Okay," Michael started to get up. He held his lower back with one hand and leaned on the arm of the chair with the other. "I know you'll do what's best for you and Rosie. It was on my mind for a while, so I thought I'd talk to you about it."

"I understand, Dad."

"I'll go back there now and relieve your mother. She mentioned something about lunch when we were on our way to pick you two up."

Mira watched him slowly make his way to the master bedroom. She was grateful that her father had cultivated such a good relationship with his grandchildren—unlike anything she had ever experienced with him as a child. There was something about him, however, since his recent retirement that made her wonder and even slightly worry about him at times. An inner nudge was telling her that it wasn't because he was simply getting older, but that there was something more to it.

3

"I'm about to make some sandwiches. Wanna help?" Sara was tying her apron in the kitchen.

"Sure, Mom." Mira proceeded over to a side table and grabbed the freshly baked bread sitting on a silver pan.

"When did you bake this?" She started slicing the loaf.

"A few hours ago. It's not so warm anymore, huh?"

"No, but surely smells tasty."

Sara retrieved the cold cuts from the refrigerator.

"Are you sure Dad's okay, Mom?"

"He's doing fine, dear, except for the back pain he whines about occasionally," Sara affirmed.

Mira sat on one of the stools next to the counter and helped her mother make the sandwiches.

"What makes you wonder?" Sara looked at her.

"I don't know. He just seems a little different— mellower I guess."

"Well, that should be expected. Your father's not as young as he used to be. People do tend to get mellower as they age. Don't you think I have?"

"No, Mom. I think not." Mira smirked.

Sara chuckled.

"So any new prospects lately?" Sara kept her eyes on the sandwich she was preparing.

Mira looked at her mother cross-eyed. "What do you mean by *prospects*?"

"You know... you met anyone special yet?"

"Mom, must we always have this conversation? You ask me the same thing at least every three months."

"That's because, you know…you're twenty-eight now, sweet pea and I think it's time that you settled down with someone nice."

"Is this a conspiracy with you and Dad?"

"What do you mean?"

"Dad questioned me about whether I'm going back to school or not and now, in the same hour, you're asking me about my love life."

"There's no conspiracy, dear." Sara's eyes met hers. "But do you have one?"

"What?" Mira scowled. "Do I have what?"

"A love life."

Mira sighed hopelessly.

"Bobby Newton's been asking about you a lot lately."

"For what?"

"He's been a little subtle about it at first," Sara went on, "but I notice that every time you come home to visit, he makes it a point to come see you. He's also been helping your father out in the yard most weekends and helps us with practically anything else we might need."

"Really?" Mira asked.

"Really."

"Why didn't you tell me he was keeping you guys so hot?"

"Well, I'm telling you now." Sara stopped what she was doing and leaned over the counter. "One day, I came right out and asked him."

"Pray tell, what?" Mira was gearing up for the disclosure.

"If he liked you."

"Mom...you didn't!"

"I certainly did!" Sara straightened up again. "It was obvious that he did and I could see that he was just too shy to reveal it."

"What did he say?"

"Do you really want to know?" Sara seemed eager.

Mira thought for a moment and sighed again. "To be honest with you, Mom... No, I don't really wanna know. Bobby's a nice guy and all, but I'm not interested. I just wanna focus on me and Rosie. I don't have any room in my life for a relationship."

Sara's heart sank. "Mira!"

"What?"

"How can you say that? That you don't have any room in your life for a relationship? Don't you want to settle down with someone you can share your life with and grow old together with?"

"I can do that with my daughter, Mom."

"Now, that answer was just plain silly!" Sara's hands were at the waist.

"Not to me."

"For your information, dear, Rosie is going to grow up someday and meet a nice, handsome fella of her own. She's not going to court you, my dear. She'll have her own life to live." She leaned over the counter again. "Look…you've known Bobby ever since grade school and you two have always gotten along so well. Why not give him a chance? He is interested; he straight out told me."

Mira was quiet. Sara could tell that she was analyzing all of the information.

"I'm not interested, Mom," she finally replied.

Sara exhaled heavily. "I can't believe you, Mira!" She was shaking her head. "No man's ever going to be good enough for you. I'm right. Ain't I?"

"I don't know what you're talking about. Why are you making such a big deal of this anyway?" Mira was becoming agitated. "I'm a grown woman now, Mom. If I choose to be by myself for the rest of my life, that's my prerogative. I'm not saying that's what I want. It's just that…"

"No one can ever fit the bill," Sara interjected. "You know what I'm talking about."

"I have no idea, Mom. I really don't."

Sara walked around the counter and sat next to Mira. "Every single fella I knew that showed the slightest interest in you, you push them away."

"You've lost me there."

"Take Rosie's father, for instance. The guy just forgot your birthday and you dumped him!"

"Mother, for your information, Cody and I had been dating for a full two years. There was no excuse for him not to remember my birthday," Mira countered. "Furthermore, it was more than just that."

"Sweet pea, you know that's all it was. Cody was a real gentleman who treated you so well the time you were together. No amount of calls or pleading on his part prompted you to take him back after you broke up with him. I never understood how you could do that."

"You weren't in the relationship with him, Mom. You couldn't see his stupid flaws. Furthermore, if he was such a nice guy and a *gentleman* as you say, how come after he saw that I wasn't getting back with him, he moved away and seemingly forgot he had a daughter. Such a nice guy he is!"

"You're right about that," Sara agreed. "He's so wrong and he'll regret that one day, but let's not make this about Cody…I'm talking about you. Ever since that incident with Karlen Key and Andy all those years ago, you've taken on the viewpoint that love relationships must be perfect—like theirs was."

"I really don't know what you're talking about." Mira looked away momentarily.

"Don't you remember what you said to me that very evening after Karlen and Andy were re-united?"

"No."

"I remember. You said that when you grew up, you would never fall in love with a man if he wasn't like Andy."

"The revelation instantly jogged Mira's memory."

"You said that he was the perfect man and you wanted to have a relationship just like theirs when you grew up," Sara continued.

Mira was silent.

"I think I understand now. You don't think you've found the man that's measured up to the standards you've set based on those qualities you saw in Andy."

"That's ridiculous," Mira finally responded.

"No, it's not and you know I'm right, dear. I realize that experience you had all those years ago - witnessing the extremely passionate, undying love they had for one another made a lasting imprint in your young mind of what love between a couple should be like. But sweetheart, I'm going to be honest with you... Romantic relationships require work. When the butterflies in the stomach settle down, couples tend to come back to reality. The struggles, hardships and disagreements set in and if the love is true and pure from the beginning, it can survive. What you didn't see were the struggles, hardships and disagreements Karlen and Andy might have had with each other when they were courting. You didn't see the attitudes and personalities that clashed from time to time. You just saw the most meaningful part—which is how strong and lasting their love was that even transcended death and that's what was so beautiful and gave you the outlook on life you have today."

"I don't know, Mom. You've arrived at such a deep conclusion to a simple matter," Mira said.

Sara gently stroked her daughter's hair, then got up and walked back around the counter.

"Just think about what I said. I know when you and your brother were younger, you didn't see much affection coming my way from your father and I know that's not what you want for your life. But you know your father is a different man now and these past fifteen years have made up for all the years prior to that. He's more loving, affectionate and although he's still not much of a talker, he communicates way more than he used to. Our love may not be a fairy-tale type of romance, but it's true love and as we're growing old together, we're both grateful that we're here for each other and enjoying life. That's what I want for you—

someone you can share your life with in a loving, caring way." She placed two sandwiches on a tray. "I'm going to take these to your father and Rosie."

Mira sat at the kitchen counter, surprised that her mother had even brought up the Karlen and Andy saga.

She pulled up one of the sandwiches and took a bite. Her mother was beginning to get inside her head. *Maybe she's right*, she thought. Then in a split second, she decided that she still felt the same way as before and nothing her mother said was going to change that.

That night…

Mira was helping Rosie with her pajama top. The little one had just finished her bubble bath.

"Why do you always do this, Mom? I'm old enough to do it myself," Rosie stated matter-of-factly.

Just then, Sara appeared at the door. "So you're ready for bed now, huh?"

"Yes, Nana," Rosie answered cheerfully. "Umm…Nana, may I watch one more program with Pops before I go to sleep?"

"Now, pumpkin…" Sara stepped further into the room, "…that's completely up to your mother." She glanced at Mira.

"Mom, can I?" Rosie made her plea.

"Honey, it's late. It's actually almost ten o'clock now." Mira glanced at the clock affixed to the wall. "You and Dad have watched television for hours already. Dad has to get some sleep and so do you. There's always tomorrow, okay?"

Sara smiled as she looked on.

"Okay, Mom." Rosie pouted a little as she climbed into bed.

Mira walked toward her mother. "Can they ever get enough of that TV?" Mira remarked. "She's not interested nearly as much when we're home."

"That's because that is their special thing," Sara responded. "Whenever your father passes on…" she lowered her voice to a whisper, "…that's most likely the thing she'll miss the most. They're creating memories that will last a lifetime. Have a good night, dear." She patted Mira's shoulder and left the room.

4

After breakfast, Rosie and her grandfather busied themselves with a game of Checkers. Mira washed the dishes, then sauntered out into the western side of the yard where her parents had placed two adjustable patio chairs side by side near the plum tree. She reached up and snatched a few plums, then stretched out in one of the tilted chairs.

As she sucked the delectable flesh of plum, the early sun met her ankles. She welcomed the warm glow that soaked through her strapped sandals.

"There you are!" Sara said. "I was wondering where you had disappeared to."

"This was really a cool idea putting these chairs in this spot." Mira spat out a seed and put another plum in her mouth.

"It's better than being on the front porch," Sara noted, sitting in the other chair. "There's no shade there, so when the sun's piping hot, you've got to get indoors unless you're looking for a tan."

There was a brief silence.

"Your father and I are taking Rosie to the theme park today. I just told her before I came out here."

"That's great. She'll love it."

"Afterwards, we're going for cake and ice-cream. I haven't told her that part yet, though," Sara giggled.

"You're trying to do all of that today?" Mira asked.

"Sure. Why not? We'll leave around noon, so we'll have plenty of time to get everything in."

"I just think it's a lot for you and Dad to do. You'll most likely be at the park for hours and after that, you'll all be tired—except maybe for Rosie. Whenever I go there, the only thing I wanna do right after is come home and go to sleep."

"That's because you young people are not as strong sometimes as us older folks. Wiser, but weaker..."

"Sure, Mom," Mira smirked.

"I took these two weeks' vacation because I wanted to spend as much time as I can with you guys and I plan to get in as much fun time as possible. I thought Rosie was excited about going to the theme park, but your father is even more excited than she is!"

A sudden burst of laughter escaped the house. "I win! I win!" They heard Rosie exclaim.

Mira and Sara laughed.

"It's like no one else on earth matters once she's with her Pops." Sara smiled.

"So true."

At that moment, Mira's attention shifted toward the far, southern end of the street.

Sara could not help but notice the length of her daughter's stare. "Did I ever tell you that a family moved into that house?" she asked.

"What house?"

"Cornelius Ferguson's house."

Mira gaped at her mother. "Really? When?"

"A few months ago, a senator and his family moved in after fixing up the place pretty good. The house was vacant for well over a decade, so they must have had a great deal of work to get that place inhabitable. By the way, they're colored folks too," Sara noted.

Mira sat straight up—clearly stunned. "I wonder if they heard the stories."

"I have no idea. I heard the husband isn't very friendly and the wife rarely associates with anyone around here neither, so I couldn't tell you what they know."

Mira leaned slowly back again. "Well, maybe they're doing just fine at the house since Karlen's no longer there. I would think it's nice and peaceful just like any other house would be. I'm surprised that it remained empty all those years after she moved on."

"You might be forgetting, sweet pea that only a handful of people knew that Karlen moved on. People around this town fear that once a place was haunted, it's always haunted anyway, so if they knew or not, it might not have made a difference."

"Did they save most of the bearing trees?" Mira asked. "I can still see a few from here."

"Most of the trees that were there in front of the property are still there," Sara returned. "They cleared down the entrance that leads to the house starting more at the right side of where the fence used to be. I guess they didn't have the heart to uproot all those lovely, fruit-bearing trees. They did a really nice job with the driveway. You can't see it from here."

Suddenly, Mira had an idea. "Maybe Rosie and I will pay them a visit. What's their surname?"

"Benjamin, I think. Mira, you really don't want to intrude. Some people would rather be left alone." Sara seemed flabbergasted by the very idea.

"True, Mom, but I'm sure just going and introducing myself will only be interpreted as my being neighborly and nothing more."

"You're not going to mention anything; are you?"

"I… don't think so. Don't see any need for that right now," Mira replied.

Laughter erupted again from the inside. "This time you lose!" Michael blurted.

Rosie was giggling even louder than before. "I saw what you did, Pops! You cheater!"

Her words pulled Mira into a flashback of when she and Wade did anything competitively—she always accused him of cheating.

"Wade and I used to fry fish in this very spot," Mira indicated with her chin. "We never told you that."

"You didn't have to." Sara smiled. "A mother always knows when her kids are up to something even if she never breathes one word of it. I can only imagine some of the other things you and your brother got into when my and your father's backs were turned."

"I don't think you wanna know, Mom." Mira was obviously taunting her mother with curiosity.

"So, you're going to keep the rest to yourself, huh?"

"Mum's, the word."

"Well, you just go right ahead, sweet pea." Sara got up. "Have to head inside now and fold some laundry, then I'll get a little rest before it's time for us to leave. Are you coming with us?"

"I'm not sure," Mira replied. "I may just let you guys go and have fun without me. You usually do, anyway, everytime Rosie and I come down."

"Aww... such a baby. It's your own fault if your daughter thinks you're not 'fun' enough to hang with Nana and Pops."

Sara's smile was undoubtedly sickening. She cheerfully walked off and disappeared around the bend.

For the longest time, Mira sat alone thinking about the new residents of the Ferguson house. The more she thought about the prospect of going anywhere near the place again, the more interested she became. She soon got up, picked a few more plums then headed back inside. Peeking into her parents' room, she saw that her father and Rosie had quieted down and were watching television together in bed.

"What's on?" She stood at the door with arms folded.

"The Friendly Ghost." Rosie glanced up at Mira. She was lying on her stomach in the opposite direction of her grandfather with her face cupped inside her little hands. Michael was resting on his back with fingers interlocked behind his head.

"Don't you ever get tired of scary pictures?" Mira asked Rosie.

Michael laughed. "Did *you* ever get tired of them when you were her age?"

"Dad!"

"What?" Michael looked her way.

"I didn't want her to know I did the same thing!" She spoke in a coarse whisper.

"I hear you, Mom," Rosie sang.

Michael sighed. "Does she ever have bad dreams after watching supposed scary pictures?" he asked Mira.

"No."

"Well, leave her be! She's a tough kid. What might give you the shakes, probably won't faze her."

Mira walked in and sat next to Rosie. "Wanna go for a walk?"

"Now?" Rosie inquired.

"Yeah, but I can wait until your picture's over if you want."

Rosie looked back at her grandfather. He could tell she was wondering if he would be disappointed if she left.

"Go ahead. We have a full two weeks to watch TV together," Michael assured her.

"Okay, Pops!" She scooted up and kissed him on the cheek. Mom and I won't be long. Would we, Mom?"

"No sweetheart. We won't be long."

"Okay then. I'll put on my shoes and make sure my hair is fixed nicely."

"Good girl," Mira said as Rosie skipped out of the room. "What on earth have you done to her, Dad?"

Michael arched his brows. "Me? I haven't done a thing."

"That child doesn't wanna spend a good minute apart from you when she's here. It's crazy, you know?"

Michael only smiled.

"Nana! Mom and I are going for a walk!" Rosie exclaimed while darting past Wade's old room. Sara had been putting away the folded clothes.

"So, you're really going there? Aren't you?" Sara appeared at the bedroom door, moments later. She was looking at Mira intently.

A tad confused, Michael glanced at them both.

"I told you I was, Mom. You thought I was kidding?"

"Going where?" Michael had to know.

"Mira's going over to the Ferguson house," Sara filled him in.

"What on earth for?" Michael sat up, grimacing from the slight pain he suddenly felt in his back. "Don't people live there now— a politician and his family?"

"Dad, I'm only going to be neighborly and introduce myself," Mira said.

"And you're taking Rosie with you." Sara's voice held a tinge of disdain.

"Why not? We could both do with the walk and Rosie loves meeting people," Mira returned.

"I still don't think you should intrude. Don't you agree, Michael?"

Michael attempted to lie down again. "She says she's just going to hail. I don't see any harm in that," he replied.

"See, Mom. There's no harm in that." Mira smiled as her mother turned away from the door.

As Mira led the way toward the end of the street, Rosie skipped happily along. She was wearing a pink skirt that stopped just above the knees and a matching blouse. Those beloved candy curls of hers bounced up and down and around her face, glistening in the sun.

"May I have a mango?" she asked as they approached the edge of the Ferguson property.

Mira stared up at the tall mango tree just ahead whose branches were stretched long and wide. The tree was stacked with fruit and as much as she wanted to please her daughter, Mira knew she was no climber. How she wished right then that Wade was there—the designated climber.

She scanned the ground that was visited by a variety of multi-colored leaves and dry limbs of all sizes which had dropped from the various trees. She was hoping to find something long enough to reach the mangos. Then several feet over to her left, she found the perfect branch. Though it had withered to a noticeable degree, Mira deemed it strong enough to propel a mango from its stem. Stretching up onto her toes, the edge of the branch barely touched the mangos, but with one hard swing forward in union with a slight leap, one of them fell helplessly to the ground and Rosie hurried over to pick it up.

"Mom, you've got it! Thanks!"

Mira dropped the branch. "You're welcome, honey."

She looked over to the edge of the asphalt driveway that led to the house she had deliberately avoided over the years. The house still could not be seen from the road and as Mira moved in that direction, it was apparent that the Benjamins had not altered much of the yard. It looked pretty much the way it did all those years ago except for the long, curvy driveway which led up to the house. The house! It was magnificent! Mira held Rosie's hand as they walked the property.

"Mom, why are we here?" Rosie asked.

"We're just going to pay some nice people a visit," Mira replied, utterly entranced by the huge makeover the house had undertaken—which once had broken windows on every side, peeling paint all over and missing doors. It had been delightfully transformed into a rose-colored, colonial-style edifice with tall, white columns in front, clean, beautiful windows and decorative window frames. Mira was convinced that the Ferguson house was now as charmingly captivating as it probably was when Cornelius and his wife, Marlena, lived there over a century before.

"This house is so pretty, Mom," Rosie commented.

"It sure is, honey."

It took a few minutes for them to get to the front porch that was neatly covered with large, white and beige interlocking marble tiles. Mira felt fairly strange standing in front of the darkly-stained double doors that weren't there at her last visit.

"Aren't you going to knock?" Rosie looked up at her mother who was still holding her hand, but staring quietly ahead.

"Ah...yes. I'll ring the door-bell." Mira reached over and pressed the small button next to the door.

They soon heard the pitter-patter of feet.

"I'll get it!" a little voice cried.

"Oh, no you won't!" A man's voice quickly followed.

The door flashed open and standing on the opposite side was a medium-framed colored man with very low hair and a neatly-trimmed moustache. His face was smooth and clear, and he looked 'rich' — in Mira's estimation. Behind him was a slender lady, a few inches taller than he was, who had a narrow, sunken face and shoulder-length, black hair. Standing next to the man was a young boy, probably around five years old, clutching a brown teddy bear. He was wearing a white onesie that had seen some spills a few inches under the boy's chin.

"May I help you?" the man asked Mira quite nobly after making brief eye-contact with Rosie.

"Hi, my name is Mira Cullen and this is my daughter, Rosie." She paused for a moment, which was met with utter silence. "Um, I live…I used to live just down the street there. My parents are actually still there—the Cullens…"

Silence again and a penetrating stare emerged from the gentleman.

"I heard that someone had moved here and we just decided to come and introduce ourselves, and welcome you to the neighborhood."

"Well, isn't that something," the man glanced back at the woman with a wide smile. "This nice, young lady and her daughter came to welcome us to the neighborhood. Isn't that something?"

At the moment, the woman's face was void of expression.

"Where did you say you live, young lady?" he asked Mira, a smile still splattering his face.

Unsure of what to make of his glee, Mira responded: "I didn't say, but I live in California. I grew up in this neighborhood."

"Oh, I see," the man replied. "Well, my hat's off to you and your little daughter because you two are the first to even bother coming this way in the six months we've been here. Would you like to come in for a minute?" He gestured with his hand.

Mira looked at Rosie, then back at him. "Sure, why not?" she replied.

"Mira…you said is your name?"

"Yes, sir."

"Mira, this is my wife, Andrea and our son, Alex. My name is Theo and our last name is Benjamin. Kindly have a seat."

"Nice to meet you all," Mira said.

She and Rosie were led over to the large living room that she remembered from before. The interior of the house was even more grandeur and exquisite than the exterior. Emerald-green marble tiles stretched magnanimously across the vast floor and tall angelic figurines graced two corners of the living room, each near a window. A rectangular, glass table, sitting elegantly on a large-sized, oriental area-rug graced the center of the room and darkly-stained wood that framed the couch and sofas were intricately designed and fit for royalty.

Rosie sat quietly next to her mother as they both felt rather out of place. The Benjamins all sat on the long, white couch on the opposite side of the table.

"May I offer you something to drink?" Andrea Benjamin asked them in a very soft voice.

"I'm fine; thank you," Mira replied. She looked at Rosie. "Sweetheart, would you like something?"

"Yes, Ma'am." She swung her tiny feet slightly as the little boy gazed at her from his mother's side.

"I have punch. Do you like punch?" The woman stood up.

"Yes, ma'am," Rosie answered shyly.

"Mama, I want punch too," the boy inserted.

"Come in the kitchen for yours, baby. Would you like to come too, Rosie?" she asked.

"Yes, ma'am," went Rosie again, getting up off the chair and following them.

"So, you say you grew up around here," Theo said to Mira, his legs now crossed and he was leaning back slightly.

"Yes I did. At eighteen, I moved away for college."

"That's nice. Which college did you attend?"

"Bensuren in L.A. They had a good Pre-med program."

"So, you studied medicine. That's very impressive. Should I be calling you Doctor Cullen?"

Mira was a little embarrassed. "Actually, I didn't finish. I kind of got pregnant and put my studies on hold."

Theo leaned forward. "Your daughter... how old is she?"

"She's six and a half," Mira answered.

"Why haven't you gone back in six and a half years? How long does it take you to bounce back in the game after a little falling out?"

"Pardon me?" Mira knew exactly what he meant.

"Why haven't you gone back to college?"

"I'm working on that, sir." She was smiling.

"Why are you smiling? Did I say something... funny?"

"No sir, not at all," Mira quickly returned. "You just remind me of my father, that's all. He had pretty much the same line of questioning for me yesterday."

"Wise man. Listen here, young lady. If you don't already know, I'm a state senator. I graduated from Trunket University with honors. I said that to say this... If I could have gotten to and through university with all the odds that were against me as a young, black man, you certainly can surpass whatever challenges you face and finish your education."

"Yes, sir," Mira replied humbly. She knew he was right—just as she knew her father was.

Just then, Andrea and the kids re-entered the room. The trace of red punch encircled Rosie and Alex's lips.

"I didn't want them to bring the punch in here, so I let them drink it in the dining room." Andrea said as she took a seat next to her husband again.

"Mama, can I show Rosie my toys upstairs?" Alex asked.

Andrea was obviously unsure and looked Mira's way for approval.

Mira turned to Rosie. "If the Benjamins don't mind, you can go."

"Why, of course we don't mind!" Andrea stated. The children started taking off toward the long, winding staircase. "You kids just be careful going up the stairs," Andrea warned.

"You all have done a beautiful job with this house," Mira noted, looking at the staircase that she vividly recalled barely getting to the top of years earlier, but sprinting down like lightning after spotting Karlen in the master closet.

The Benjamins had clearly done an overhaul to the staircase and replaced the rusty, tattered rail with a shiny, black, decorative one.

"Thank you," Theo replied. "The renovations, as you probably can imagine, were massively expensive considering the fact that the house was already very old and uninhabited for many years."

"Might I presume by your compliment that you were here before—inside I mean?" Andrea posed.

Mira looked away for a second to retrieve the correct response, then her eyes met Andrea's again. "Yes. My brother and I explored this property when we were kids."

"Really?" Theo's eyes widened. "You weren't scared?"

"Pardon me?" Mira was feeling like she was being thrown a curve ball.

"Didn't you hear the rumors about this place?" Theo returned.

"Um…at one point we did, but it wasn't until after we had already stopped by."

Mira noticed a seemingly hopeful beam in Andrea's eyes just then. She wasn't sure why, but the woman's entire facial expression suddenly relaxed.

Theo was laughing. "Folks around these parts make mountains out of molehills. They stretch the truth and concoct urban legends and folk tales that are nowhere near reality." He shifted a bit in his seat and glanced at his wife. "I can't tell you the number of folks who thought we were absolutely out of our minds for even thinking of purchasing this place. Every one of them tried to talk us out of it, but..." he looked around proudly at the place, "...the price was right and the house had potential. There was no way I was going to allow some hocus pocus made-up tale of this being a haunted house cause me to pass up on that offer."

Andrea was silent, but Mira could tell by her demeanor that something wasn't right.

"Am I right, honey?" Theo asked Andrea.

"Yes, dear," was her stoic reply.

Mira then glanced at her watch. "Oh, we must be going now. My parents are taking Rosie to the theme park today."

That's so nice," Andrea remarked. "How long are you and your daughter here for?"

"Two weeks," Mira replied.

"Okay. Well, hopefully, we'll see you and Rosie again before you leave," Theo said.

"I'm sure you will. Thanks so much for the hospitality."

"No, no… you're the hospitable one. Like I said earlier, you and your daughter are the first to even bother coming around. It was indeed a pleasure meeting you both." Theo smiled.

They all stood up and Mira walked over to the foot of the staircase and called out to Rosie. She came down moments later.

"Mom, can I stay for a while longer?" she asked with that pleading look again. Alex was standing next to her—also hopeful.

"Rosie, you know you're going out with Pops and Nana today."

"Just a little while longer, Mom? Alex and I were having so much fun. He lets me play with all his toys!"

"You can always bring her back another time, Mira," Andrea interjected. "I'm here practically all day, every day and I'll be happy to have little Rosie come by at any time. I know we don't know each other, but I can assure you that she'll be in good hands."

Mira looked at Rosie again whose plea she found difficult to resist. "Would you like to come by tomorrow if that's okay with Mrs. Benjamin?" she asked.

"Tomorrow will be fine with me," Andrea responded.

"Yes, Mom. I would love to," Rosie replied.

"Yay!" Alex beamed from ear to ear.

"Well then...it's settled," Theo chimed in.

The Benjamins walked Mira and Rosie to the door.

"It was really a pleasure meeting you all," Mira said on the front porch.

The Benjamins were standing almost in the exact, same spots as they were when the door first opened.

As Mira turned to leave, Rosie's eyes were diverted directly behind where Andrea stood. Theo glanced back to the area of her gaze, then looked back at Rosie. "We'll see you later, Rosie. You and your mom take care now." He shut the door.

"I was having so much fun with Alex, Mom!" Rosie exclaimed as they headed down the long driveway. "He's a great kid and he has the coolest toys."

"That's really nice to know." Mira smiled.

"Mom, who was that man standing behind Alex's parents just now before we left?"

"A man? I didn't see anyone, sweetheart. Are you sure you saw someone?"

"I guess. He was really tall and looked like Santa Claus."

"Maybe it's a guest of theirs we didn't meet or someone who works for them."

"Perhaps. It's a shame he didn't introduce himself. Isn't it, Mom?"

"Yes. When we go back tomorrow, we'll probably get to meet him," Mira replied.

* * *

You two have finally found your way back," Sara said as the pair entered through the kitchen door. She was making tea. "So, how did it go? What type of people are they? Are they friendly?" she riddled off.

Mira sat at the counter while Rosie rushed to the back of the house.

"Rosie, dear, your bath water is waiting. We have to leave soon!" Sara cried behind her granddaughter.

"Yes, Nana!"

"The Benjamins seem like really nice people," Mira said as her mother listened intently. They invited us inside and we had a good conversation while Rosie and their son played upstairs for a while."

"Really?"

"You know, I found out that no one other than Rosie and I had ever bothered to welcome them to the neighborhood. I wonder why that is, Mom."

Sara's face was contorted to a slight grimace. "Do you think we avoided them because of...? You can't possibly think..."

"You tell me, Mom. I don't even know how anyone around here could conceive that they're not friendly people if no one has ever met them."

"Mira, the reason no one has bothered to meet them, dear, is because no one wants to go anywhere near that house. You know the place was haunted," Sara replied.

"Was, Mom. It *was* haunted. You and I both know that it's not anymore. So even you had no excuse for not being neighborly."

Sara sighed and placed both hands on the counter. "Sweet pea, even though Karlen Key found her way out of that place, it was no telling if anything remained. That's how I always saw it and that's why your father and I never had any reason to re-visit it under any circumstances. You know people in this town are quite superstitious and anything that carried any type of paranormal energy is something they avoid like a plague. I'm pretty sure that no one was avoiding the Benjamins for any other reason than that and you of all people and your brother know that your father and I are not racists."

"I know, Mom. I guess that explains it then. But yeah... they seem like very nice people and come to think of it, they might understand why they haven't had any neighbors show up to the house. Mister Benjamin did mention that everyone thought they were crazy for living there."

"You see?"

"Yeah. By the way, Rosie wants to go over and play with the little boy again, so Mrs. Benjamin agreed that she can come back tomorrow for a while."

Sara was surprised. The expression on her face did not conceal that fact.

"Without you?"

"Yes, without me."

"Are you sure it's a good idea?" Sara pressed.

"Yes, why wouldn't it be?"

"I don't know. I just don't like that house." She shook her head. "It's probably my superstitious mind taking over again." She picked up her tea. "Well, we have to get going soon, so I'll go and check on Rosie and we should be out of here in less than an hour."

"Hey...why don't you let me deal with Rosie and you can just finish getting ready?"

"No, that's okay. I've got everything covered."
She smiled and walked off.

5

Mira stood at the kitchen door watching as her dad reversed the car down the driveway. Rosie was waving goodbye to her from the back seat in between both grandparents. Mira waved back, amazed at how her little girl absolutely refused that she join them on their soon-to-be fabulous outing. The unspoken rules were clear: A visit to Mizpah meant 'Pops, Nana and Rosie time' and that was basically the sum of it.

Mira locked the screen door behind her, then went over and flopped onto the couch—something her mother detested seeing them do to the furniture when she and Wade were younger. It was a trait that followed her as an adult and seemingly no amount of verbal chastisement from her mother or frowns that accompanied them swayed her to do any better.

She switched on the old, box television that sat faithfully in that space for nearly a decade. Although the house was now in its golden years, Mira admired how her mother still kept it in tip-top condition, spic and span—just as she always did when they were children.

As she watched the comedian on TV running from his wife who was after him with a large skillet, Mira felt a warm, inviting sleep coming on, and before she knew it, she had quietly drifted off into dreamland.

What felt like hours later, she pitched up from sleep as she heard someone knocking at the kitchen door.

Who the hell is that? She wondered, sluggishly making her way over to the door. "All right, I'm coming!"

When she observed through the screen that it was Bobby Newton, she almost sucked her teeth out loud. With sheer hesitance, she twisted the lock and opened up.

"Hi, Bobby." Her voice was coldly monotonous.

"Hey, Mira. I…I heard you were in town, so I thought I'd stop by and give you a hail."

She was simply looking at him. His gray eyes appeared so innocent, yet entrancing enough that she could not possibly deny that the baby-faced stud standing before her with the tight abs, muscular physique, short, spiky brown hair and perfectly-chiseled face would be almost any girl's dream. Yet, by the same token, she knew that he wasn't hers.

"Um…"

"You wanna sit for a while out back?" she interrupted.

"Uh…sure."

With hands shoved deeply inside the pockets of his shorts, Bobby followed Mira around to the side of the house where the plum tree and lawn chairs were.

She wasted no time sitting down and stretching back while Bobby took the seat next to her.

"So where's Rosie?" he asked.

"She's out with my parents."

Suddenly, she released a heavy sigh and with eyes fixated straight ahead, she said, "Let's cut the crap, Bobby. You knew exactly where Rosie was before you asked that question. Mom called you before she left, didn't she?"

Bobby was evidently taken aback as guilt quickly shrouded his face. However, he was aware that the bluntness of her tone was just Mira being Mira. "Um…yes." He held his head down like a puppy dog.

She looked at him. "What's with you two anyway?"

"Who? Your Mom and me?"

"Yeah. Why are you practically the topic of conversation every time I come back home?"

Bobby grinned shyly. "I guess it's because I see them a whole lot these days."

Mira shifted to her side. "I hear you've been helping around here a bit—Dad with the yard work."

"Yeah." He grinned again. "Your dad really loves his yard work. He only allows me to do so much, though."

"Thanks." A soft expression formed.

"For what?"

"Helping my dad."

"Oh, that's nothing. He's a great guy; been nothing but kind to me. Did you know he linked me up with that job at the Mill?"

"No, I didn't know that," Mira replied.

"I was down on my luck at that time and good-paying jobs around here were pretty scarce. Your dad looked out for me, so I feel greatly indebted to him. Furthermore, I recently got promoted and now I'm taking up some courses at the Community College a few evenings every week. All thanks to your dad."

"That's impressive, Bobby. Congrats on your promotion."

This time, he blushed.

"So, I thought that since your father always did his own yard work on the weekends, I'd pop by and help him out," Bobby added.

"That's really sweet of you," Mira said. "Dad's older now and I know he refuses to entertain the notion that he can't do quite as much as he used to before. He can be stubborn sometimes."

"You're telling me? I have to pretty much fight to convince him to let me do the heavier work. He

70

thinks he can handle it, but I've been seeing how much his back has been bothering him lately and my conscience wouldn't allow me to stand by and let him do it."

Mira shifted on her back again. "Dad's been on me lately about going back to college."

Bobby's ears were perked. "Are you gonna?"

"Eventually. I have a really good job right now with great benefits, so I don't feel the need to rush anything. I'll go back at the right time."

There was a little silence, then Bobby cleared his throat as if something was actually stuck inside of it, yet nothing but pure nervousness prevailed.

"I…I was wondering if you'd like to have lunch with me tomorrow or we can go for a couple of cones instead," he stated apprehensively.

Mira was looking into space, obviously giving his proposal some thought.

"If you'd rather not, I understand." Bobby needed to break the ice that had quickly surrounded him.

"I'd like that…lunch, I mean," Mira answered.

"What?"

"I said, *yes*, Bobby—I'll have lunch with you."

He was now smiling from ear to ear, his face alight with overwhelmingly relief. "Oh, that's…that's great!" The excitement was clear from Mira's point of view. "Would one o'clock be okay? You can bring Rosie along if you want."

"Yeah. I'll see about that."

"Sorry?"

"My daughter's stuck to my dad's ribcage, so I don't know if she'll be the least bit interested in coming with us. Maybe if she hears 'ice cream', she'll at least think about it," Mira replied.

Bobby smiled.

"Oh, by the way, I just remembered something. Rosie's going over to a neighbor's house tomorrow, so she definitely won't be coming with us. She's met a new friend named Alex and is really looking forward to spending some time over at his house with his mom."

"I see. Well then, it'll just be you and me," Bobby declared with immense anticipation.

"I guess," Mira said stoically. She felt it was the least she could do for the poor guy who was so good to her father. Nothing more, nothing less.

"So are you having a great time today?" Sara asked Rosie. They were sitting at the front window of the ice cream parlor at a beautifully glazed, circular table. Rosie had just taken a huge lick of her ice cream cone.

"I had a blast, Nana!" she managed a response with some of the butter pecan still caked up on her tongue. "And this ice cream's great too!"

Michael and Sara laughed.

"I'm glad you're enjoying yourself, pumpkin." Sara put her elbows on the table and rested her chin atop interlaced knuckles.

Michael suddenly grimaced as he pressed onto his left, lower back.

"Are you all right, honey?" Sara asked.

He glanced at Rosie and saw the concern in her eyes. "Yeah, I'm fine. Probably just a pinched nerve or something."

"Are you sure, Pops?" Rosie asked.

"I'm doubly sure, pumpkin," Michael nodded with a smile.

The little girl continued licking her ice cream—this time, not saying very much.

6

Mira and Rosie made the long walk up the Benjamin's driveway the following morning. The child had stuffed a few play items in her backpack that she was eager to share with Alex. Mira noticed that, unlike the other day, only one car sat in the driveway. It was a shiny, black Cadillac with a convertible top. The emerald green Buick was missing.

She stooped down and checked Rosie's face again after ringing the doorbell.

"Oh, hi. You've arrived!" Andrea said upon opening the door. A plain, burgundy dress with short sleeves was partially hidden behind her pink and white floral apron. Alex was standing excitedly next to his mother.

"Yes, Ma'am," Rosie replied softly, glancing shyly at Alex.

"Hi, Mrs. Benjamin. I hope we're not too early. Hi Alex." Mira smiled.

The little boy waved his hand cheerfully.

"By no means are you too early," Andrea replied. "Come on in, Rosie."

Mira kissed Rosie on the cheek as she released her hand.

"Bye, Mom. Love you!" The little girl hurried inside to join Alex.

"Have you had breakfast yet? I made pancakes," Andrea asked Rosie who then looked back at her mother.

"Can I, Mom?"

Andrea seemed puzzled.

"Yes, you may, Rosie," Mira answered. She looked at Andrea. "She's had breakfast already, but she always manages to find space for pancakes whenever the opportunity presents itself. She absolutely loves them."

"Oh, I see why she asked you!" Andrea chuckled.

"Yes, Ma'am."

"Well, would you like to come in for coffee or tea?"

"I would love to, but I have to help my mother with a few chores," Mira explained.

"All right. Well then...I'll see you later. Don't worry about Rosie; she'll be fine."

"I'm sure she will. Thank you so much for having her come over, Mrs. Benjamin. I'll be back for her in a few hours."

"You take your time, dear." Andrea smiled. She watched Mira descend the porch steps, then she quietly closed the front door.

Andrea followed the children who had already taken their seats at the breakfast table. "Alright then. Let's dig in, people!" she said, sitting down and dishing up pancakes for the kids. Rosie was already feeling quite at home and was anxious to show Alex her toys.

About twenty minutes later, Andrea told them: "Wash your hands before heading upstairs, okay?"

"Yes, Ma'am," Alex and Rosie responded simultaneously.

They hurried into the downstairs bathroom and Rosie waited while Alex quickly washed up. From her peripheral vision, she thought she had seen someone pass by in a dark suit.

"Is your dad here?" she asked.

"No. He left a little while ago," Alex moved away from the faucet so that she could get her turn. He dried his hands on the large towel nearby and scooted out of the bathroom.

"Meet me upstairs!" he cried, darting up the winding staircase.

"Okay!" Rosie yelled back, quickly rinsing the few remaining suds from her hands.

She too dashed out of the bathroom, then stopped abruptly as blocking her passage in front of the staircase was a tall man with white hair and a short distinctive moustache. He was dressed in a black coat suit that appeared to be older in style than what she was accustomed to seeing, and he wore shiny, black shoes.

He was distinguished-looking. It was the same man she had seen when she and her mother were leaving the day before.

"I'm sorry. I shouldn't have been running." She lowered her head with guilt.

The man slowly folded his hands in front. "That is quite all right, little girl. I'm Mister Koney. What's your name?" he asked.

"Nice to meet you, Mister Koney." She looked up again. "I'm Rosie. I'm just visiting today."

"Nice to meet *you*, Rosie." He stepped graciously aside with a nod—an invitation she took to proceed upstairs.

Alex was already in the process of sifting through his toy box when Rosie stepped inside the room. Let's play with my robot! His name's John. You want to?" he asked, stretching out his hand with the twelve-inch tall robot suited in military-like armor.

"Yeah, that's cool!" Rosie gladly accepted and straightaway twisted the twining mechanism at its side and placed it onto the floor. They gleefully watched it march up and down the room until it died down completely and Alex went over to restart.

Andrea heard the giggles upstairs while she washed the dishes.

"I brought my favorite doll," Rosie said, reaching into her backpack. "Her name's Gina. Would you like to hold her?"

Alex frowned. "I'm a boy. Boys don't play with dolls!"

"Why not? I'm playing with your robot and I'm a girl."

"Boys and girls can play with robots," Alex thought to educate her.

"Not girly girls...and I'm a girly girl."

"Who says?"

"No one, but I think since I'm playing with your toys, you should play with mine." Rosie was pouting.

"Okay, okay. I'll hold your doll for a little while, but if my Mama comes in here, I'm giving her back." He took the doll.

Rosie smiled with a real sense of achievement.

After a while, she was on the floor with the robot and a toy truck while Alex was sitting nearby changing the doll's clothes. "These are like my Mama's—only brighter." He pointed to the doll's chest.

"How do you know?" Rosie delved.

"I walked into her room one day and saw her getting dressed," the boy divulged.

"Hurry and put on her blouse before she catches a cold."

"Okay. I wouldn't want her to catch a cold. When I catch a cold, I feel so yucky." He quickly dressed the doll.

"Yeah. Me too. Take Baby out of my backpack. I think he's getting a bit warm in there," Rosie said.

"Baby?"

"Yeah. That's my teddy bear. Mom got him for me on my birthday."

Alex started searching for the bear.

"Hey, do you think your Mom or Mister Koney would like to play with us?" Rosie asked.

Alex stopped dead in his tracks. His face turned flushed. "You saw Mister Koney?"

"Yeah, downstairs. He seems awful nice."

"Oh."

"What's wrong?" Rosie noticed the sudden change of his demeanor.

"Nothing." He placed Baby on a pillow next to Gina, then climbed up onto the bed and went in a fetal position.

"Aren't you playing anymore?"

"I don't feel like it. I just want to lie down for a while," Alex replied.

"Are you sick?"

"Uh, uh." He shook his head.

"Well, you kind of look sick. I'm gonna call your mother. Mrs. Benjamin! Alex is sick!" she cried from the landing.

Rosie heard the thumping of feet mounting the staircase. Andrea entered the room moments later.

"What's the matter?" She spotted Alex in bed. "You're not feeling well, honey?"

"I'm okay, Mama," the boy replied softly.

"Are you tired?" She sat next to him and felt his fore-head.

"A little."

Andrea looked at Rosie. "Rosie, would you like to help me downstairs? We can let Alex rest for a while, then a little later, you two can play some more."

Rosie glanced at Alex. "Yes, Ma'am."

82

"Mama, I don't want Rosie to leave. Please, can she stay with me?"

Andrea stared at him for a few moments. "She would have only been gone for a little while, honey."

"No, Mama. I want her to stay!" he pleaded.

"Okay." Andrea sighed. "I'll turn on the TV for you guys. You can just watch TV for a while."

"Don't worry, Mrs. Benjamin. I'll take good care of Alex," Rosie stated—the sincerity in her voice brought about an unexpected smile to the woman's face.

Andrea patted Rosie's arm. "Thanks, dear. You're so nice." She went over and switched on the television before leaving the room.

* * *

Mira looked at her reflection in the mirror. The blue, fish-shaped, dangling earrings complimented the light-blue pants outfit she was wearing. She was ready to go and expected Bobby to show up at any minute. Her mother was elated when she heard they were actually going on a date, although Mira made it clear to her that it wasn't a real date - just lunch.

83

"What are you doing?" She shook her head slowly, still staring back at herself. *"You know you don't want to give him any false hope."* With that, Mira heard a vehicle pull up in front of the yard. She snatched her purse from the bed and headed out front. The car door slammed shut and she arrived at the kitchen door just before Bobby had a chance to knock.

"Hi. Wow!" Bobby said with a surprised look smothering his face. "You look…very nice."

"Thanks," Mira answered squarely. "We ought to get going."

As she went to lock the door behind them, they heard a car pull up on the driveway.

"It's your folks," Bobby said.

He and Mira watched as Sara got out from the driver's side and went over to help Michael out of the car. She placed his arm across her shoulder and started to walk with him. Bobby rushed over to help. He took the other side.

"What's wrong?" Mira asked, quickly re-opening the door of the house.

Michael looked extremely lethargic and his eyes had a slightly pink hue that Mira hadn't seen before.

"Your father is just a little tired right now, honey," Sara replied. "We're going to get him inside and tucked into bed."

"But it's so early in the day. Dad, are you all right?"

Michael nodded, but didn't say a word. Mira followed as they helped him to his bedroom. Bobby returned to the living room, moments later, and sat down on the couch.

"Honey, could you give me a few minutes alone with your father please?" Sara asked Mira. "I'll be right out as soon as I'm done."

Mira's silence served as an affirmative answer and Sara gently closed the door behind her. Mira heard the deadbolt click. Massaging the nape of her neck, she sauntered out to where Bobby was. "I wonder what's the matter," she said. "Dad looked so weak and out of it."

"He probably didn't get much sleep last night and just feels exhausted," Bobby submitted.

"I don't know." She sat next to him in contemplation. "He hasn't looked like himself lately and all the weight he's lost since the last time I saw him... I just don't know."

They sat quietly until they heard the bedroom door open, then shut softly again.

Sara joined them in the living room. It suddenly seemed like she bore the weight of the world on her shoulders.

"So, you two were on your way out I see?" She tried unsuccessfully to sound upbeat.

"Mom, what's wrong with Dad?" Mira cut to the chase.

"Is Rosie still at the Benjamins' house?"

"Yes," Mira quickly answered the question she knew her mother had posed to somehow avoid the previous question.

"You two are dressed up so nicely. Why don't you go on your way and we can talk when you get back, sweet pea? Your father just needs some rest and he'll be fine in a few hours. Trust me."

Mira turned to Bobby. "Bobby, I'm sorry, but I can't go."

"Mira!" Sara exclaimed.

Mira was still looking at Bobby. "If you want, we can do this another time. I'm really sorry."

"Uh...sure. Sure, we can. It's no problem." He got up. "Call me later?"

"Sure."

Sara sighed. "Bobby..."

"It's all right, Mrs. Cullen. Ya'll have a good day, now."

"You too, Son," Sara replied sadly.

After Bobby left, Mira stood up and faced her mother.

"You're keeping something from me. What's wrong with Dad?"

Mira's question was greeted by an eerie silence, then Sara turned away and sat down on the sofa. She patted the cushion next to her and Mira sat there.

"Sweet pea, there's something I need to tell you."

Mira felt her heart sinking at that moment. Her gut told her that what she was about to hear would not be good.

Sara took her daughter's hand into hers and sighed heavily. "Honey, your father is very sick. He's been for some time now."

She had Mira's full attention.

"I wanted to tell you and your brother so badly, but your father absolutely forbade me."

"Tell us what, Mom?"

Sara's expression revealed that she was searching for the 'right' words. With a look that ushered a wave of sadness in the space between them, she said: "Your father has stage four lung cancer, dear."

Mira stared back in utter shock.

"His chance for survival isn't good at all," Sara added.

"What?" Mira shook her head slowly as if trying to line up the jumbled thoughts in her mind in some particular order. "Are you saying he's going to die?"

Sara saw the tears quickly forming in her daughter's eyes, the sight of which pierced her heart. "Anything is possible, dear. By some miracle, your father could recover."

"We're not talking miracles, Mom. At this point of the illness, could Dad die? Tell me straight up 'cause I need to know!"

Sara shut her eyes, then looked at Mira again.

"Yes, honey. The tumor is malignant. The disease is terminal. I'm so sorry, honey. I'm so sorry." No longer able to hold back her own tears, she pulled Mira close and they embraced tightly. "I wanted so badly to tell you and Wade what was going on, but I couldn't dishonor your father's wishes. He didn't want anyone pitying him and was determined to only reveal what was happening once his condition started to deteriorate. I'm afraid he's at that point now."

Mira pulled away. "How long have you two been hiding this from us?" she asked.

"It's only been a few months since we found out." Sara started to dry her tears.

"But Dad's been complaining about back pain. Does that have anything to do with the cancer?"

"Yes. It's because of the size of the tumor and where it's situated. The disease has also progressed to his bones now." Sara explained.

"But how could he have lung cancer? Dad never smoked."

"You're right. He never did, but he does have a genetic predisposition to it."

"This can't be happening." Mira stood up, combing her fingers through her hair. "This just can't be happening! And regardless of what Dad wanted, how could you keep such a secret from his own children for so long?"

Sara could see that Mira's sadness was now intermingled with anger. She stood up as well.

"Mira, I know you find this difficult to understand and I'm sure your brother will too, but Michael—your dad—is my husband. We've been married for thirty years and I love him. I've loved him before you and Wade ever came along and I have to respect his wishes above all—no matter how unreasonable they seem to be. He doesn't have much time left with us and he didn't want to cause you and Wade, and the grandchildren so much sorrow before he passed. That's why he chose to wait until the time was getting closer. You may think it was quite selfish of your father, but in my eyes, it's probably the most *selfless* thing he has ever done. He did it for you all—not for himself. It's okay if you're mad at me, but don't be upset with your father."

Mira tried her best to restrain the tears, but they kept defying her. She hugged her mother again. "I'm not mad at you or Dad, Mom. I know you would never go against his wishes. I'm so sorry."

"Don't be, honey." She cupped Mira's face. "Now look. We'll all get through this together as a family, all right?"

Mira nodded. "This must have been so hard on you."

"Your father's the one who's had the toughest time. On top of dealing with the illness, he had to keep up with his 'tough guy routine' to pretend that everything was normal. Yes, it was difficult going along with that, but as I saw how hard he was trying, I couldn't allow myself to be weak, sweet pea. I had to be strong just like him."

Thinking back, Mira couldn't remember admiring her mother more than she did that day. Her mother's love for her father reminded her so much of Karlen Key's undying love for Andy. She didn't believe there was any possible way she could love her mother any more than she did already, but in that moment, it proved that she could — and she did.

Sara took Mira's hand and they sat down again. "On the way here, your father told me that it was time to let you guys know what was going on. I can't tell you how much of a relief that was. I felt a huge burden lift up off my shoulders, though simultaneously, a new one was descending because I had to break the terrible news to you and your brother."

Mira squeezed her mother's hand. "So when will you tell Wade?"

"I'll call him when I think he's home from work," Sara replied.

"What about chemotherapy? How's that been going?"

"No chemo. Your father absolutely refused. He says he's not going out feeling sicker than he already feels sometimes. After the prognosis and having been told by Dr. Leo that it was a one percent chance that he could survive the disease, your dad decided that he wasn't going to do the treatments."

"You didn't try to convince him otherwise?" Mira asked.

"I did, but he totally rejected the idea. Dr. Leo couldn't persuade him either. You know how stubborn your father can be."

"Yeah." Mira got up again.

"Where are you going?"

"For a walk."

"When are you getting Rosie?" Sara asked.

"In a while. You think Dad's asleep?"

"Yes. He took some of his prescription meds - one of them tend to make him a bit drowsy."

Mira went to the bathroom and washed her face, all the while feeling like she was in a bad dream. "Rosie..." she uttered softly, looking into the large, oval mirror. "How could I ever tell her that her Pops is dying? How could I?" She covered her face with both hands as tears streamed vigorously through the spaces of her fingers.

"Are you all right, honey?" Sara was at the door.

Mira patted her face dry. "Yes. Yes, I'm fine." She opened up and Sara could see the sadness on her face.

"Are you going to be okay?"

"Yes, I will. Right now, it's Rosie I'm worried about," Mira revealed.

"You don't have to tell her anything right now, Mira."

"You know she's very intelligent, Mom. With Dad not feeling well and looking the way he did when he walked through that door a while ago, Rosie would know that something's not right."

"I understand, but listen... your father doesn't want Rosie with this information just yet. He doesn't want to spoil her trip—the precious moments he has left with her. Just be strong for her, please. When it's time for her to be told, we'll all know."

Mira considered her mother's plea. She ultimately agreed.

* * *

The sky appeared completely starless as the moon gave off its light. An eerie stillness had found its way there once again. Lying next to her husband, Andrea Benjamin gazed outside through the open window at the blackness which seemed better to her than closing her eyes to sleep. She glanced over at Theo who had drifted off long ago into a welcoming dreamland or perhaps a dreamless sleep. How unlucky Andrea felt as night-time, as of late, had proven to be one of her greatest adversaries.

She felt a cold brush of wind sweep past her, then another, then another, but she knew it was no ordinary wind. It was them. They were there again. She inched closer to Theo and pulled the covers up above her chest.

Another passed by, then another, then another. Her head was darting in all directions hoping to get a glimpse of them, but it was too dark and she was simply too afraid to reach for the light. The last time proved a terrible mistake as the deep gash had bled profusely for the longest time. Her fear was tangible, thick and debilitating. Then…

"Ow!" she shrieked in pain.

Theo was jerked out of sleep.

"Ow!" Andrea felt another one. She was sitting up now.

After reaching for the lamp switch, Theo instantly spotted the long trail of blood that had seeped through the back of his wife's nightgown.

"Oh, no!" he quietly exclaimed. "Andrea..."

The look on her narrow face was one of consummate terror. Theo pulled the thin straps down from her shoulders and what came into view were dozens of gashes across her back, mostly around four to five inches in length—some of them completely mended, others only partially, and then there was the freshest one. "My God..." Theo was at a loss for words.

"They did it again, Theo...." Andrea sobbed. "They won't leave us alone!"

Suddenly, a blood-curdling scream escaped the vicinity of Alex's room and Theo and Andrea pitched up and shot down the hallway in the boy's direction.

On arrival at the bedroom, Theo switched on the light and Andrea flew right past him toward her son.

Alex was buried under the thin covers, shaking uncontrollably.

Andrea threw the covers off and cradled him in her arms. "What's wrong, honey?"

"I saw them Mama. Even more came this time."

Andrea glanced up at Theo.

"Saw who, Son?" Theo probed.

"You know who!" Andrea snarled. "This isn't the first time we're having this conversation."

She turned to Alex again. "Did they hurt you, honey?"

"No, Mama. They never hurt me, but he wants to… I just know it!" His eyes were glued to the closet.

Andrea and Theo's followed his.

"No one's there now, honey. They're all gone." She tried to assure the frightened child.

"But they always come back, Mama. They always come back!"

"Everything's fine. Mama and Daddy's here now." She could still see the fear in those innocent eyes of his. "Let me have a look, okay?"

"Okay," he softly consented.

Andrea pulled up Alex's shirt and carefully examined his chest, back and neck, then proceeded to the lower extremities. When she was finished, she pulled down his shirt again and breathed a sigh of relief. Theo stood nearby, silently watching.

"He hates me, Mama," Alex said.

"Who are you talking about, honey?" Andrea asked.

"Mister Koney."

Theo and Andrea glanced at each other, then re-focused on the boy.

"I don't know why he hates me."

Andrea was puzzled by the child's claims as she had no idea who this Mister Koney was.

"Don't worry, I will sleep in here with you tonight, okay?" she said.

Alex nodded.

Theo remained in the room as his wife sang softly to Alex. The child eventually drifted off to sleep in his mother's arms.

"You see what you've caused?" Andrea looked at her husband who had been strangely quiet the whole time.

"I haven't caused anything!" Theo wasted no time defending himself.

"I told you we should get out of this house. How much longer must we take this torture, Theo, and what on earth is preventing them from seriously hurting Alex? You see what they've done to me. Are you blind? What kind of man are you?!"

Theo started pacing the floor. "How do you think we'd look running out of here like a bunch of frightened idiots? What would people say?"

"You mean after they warned us not to buy this place and you pretty much laughed in their faces, huh?"

"I think you're blowing this whole matter out of proportion. Look…if this place was really haunted, why isn't anything crazy happening to me? Why am I the odd one out here?"

Alex was snoring lightly now and Andrea gently pulled the covers up to his waist. She then got up, walked over to Theo and stopped just a few inches from his face.

"You know what, Theo? I have no idea why nothing crazy is happening to you, but it doesn't make this experience any less real or frightening or torturous for Alex and me. We've been in this house for months now and from the third week, you've witnessed what they've done to me—every single night. You've heard Alex awake with ear-piercing screams and the only thing you can think of is how we'd look? Really? Are you so cold and full of yourself that you can actually entertain *denial* of the situation even for a second when the facts are staring you right in the face? Do you think I repeatedly slashed my own back while you slept? Do you think Alex and I have invented these stories about what we sense and feel?" Her eyes were welling with tears.

"We're not leaving under any circumstances, my darling," Theo replied matter-of-factly. "We've come too far in life to just give up on everything now. Look what we have here!" He extended his arms in an outward fashion. "Think of how much we've invested into this place and made it the envy of this neighborhood. How many people like us can say they own the plantation of a former slave master—one who oppressed our people and treated them like animals. Well, I'm spitting in his face now and he's probably turning over in his grave."

Andrea felt chills creep up her spine as her husband spoke those words, and in his eyes was something she had never seen before: The look of evil.

"Look at the big picture," he continued. "We've made it this far; we've defied the odds and we're living like the rich, white people now. There's no way in hell I'm giving this up!"

"I can't believe what I'm hearing." Andrea was completely disappointed. "So, you're saying to me that you will sacrifice your wife and child, the peace of your family, to make a statement to the whole of Mizpah and the world that you've made it and you've made it so far that you should be commended for not only owning, but *residing* on a former plantation? Theo, in case you didn't remember…slavery is over. It's been over for more than a hundred years. The point you feel the need to prove is senseless, uncalled for and plain stupid! I'm not going to subject Alex to this craziness anymore. If I have to, I'll find a place and we'll leave here for good."

Theo grabbed his wife by the arm.

She grimaced in pain. "Let me go this second! You're hurting me!"

Ignoring her cries, he yanked her again. This time, there was a violent glare in his eyes. "You are not taking my son anywhere and you will not step foot out of this house. How dare you defy me and threaten to bring shame to this family? I am a State senator. Have you lost your mind?"

She was struggling to break free of him, at the same time not wanting to wake the child. "I'm wondering if you've lost yours. Let me go!"

Theo looked at Alex who had shifted slightly in bed. He slowly released his grip.

"Get out of this room!" Andrea charged. "And don't you ever put your hand on me again! If you think shame would follow you if your family left you, Mister Senator, imagine the shame you'd feel if they find out that you put your hand on me like that!"

Seeing that she meant business, Theo turned and quietly left the room. Andrea shut the door behind him.

Overwhelmed with mixed emotions, she sat on the chair near the door and sobbed quietly. Feeling helpless and defeated, and also dismayed by her husband's aggressive behavior, she knew above everything that she must protect Alex—at any cost.

7

"Wade's going to try and get here by the weekend," Sara said as she and Mira sipped coffee at the kitchen counter.

"Dad's not up yet?" Mira asked.

"No. He was up for most of the night and fell off to sleep again at around four this morning."

"His back again?"

"That and the wheezing. You didn't hear it, huh?"

"No, I didn't."

"He's much better now after taking some more meds," Sara stated.

"Mom, what I don't understand is why you're playing doctor here instead of taking Dad to the hospital where he can get some real help," Mira said.

"He won't go," Sara replied. "Besides, there's really nothing much that they can do for him at this point other than chemo. Like I said, your father's not considering that option."

Rosie walked into the living room. "Morning," she said tiredly.

"Morning to you!" Sara quickly met her. "Do you want waffle pancakes this morning or you'd rather some cereal?"

"Nana, you know I hate cereal!" Rosie answered.

"I know," Sara chuckled. "I've already mixed a batch and will fry them up for you right now."

"Thanks, Nana. I'm going to tell Pops 'morning'."

"Oh no, dear," Sara quickly replied. "He's fast asleep. Let him get a little more rest, okay?"

Rosie looked at her mother who appeared to be totally out of it, but managed a half-smile anyway. "O…kay."

"Come sit here with Mom," Mira offered.

Rosie climbed up on the stool next to her.

"Did you sleep well, sweetheart?" Mira patted her knee.

"Yes, Mom. Did you?"

Mira's first thought was an honest one. However, her reply was determined to be more comforting. "I slept like a baby." She rubbed her nose to Rosie's.

The child giggled.

"Did you sleep well, Nana?" she asked as Sara poured the batch of pancake mix into the frying pan.

"Like a charm, pumpkin." She smiled lovingly.

Just then, they heard a door crack open and Michael advanced into the room. Sara quickly lowered the heat on the stove and went to meet him.

"I'm all right." He put his hand up. "Good morning, everyone."

Rosie rushed to meet him and he leaned over slightly to hug her.

Sara helped him back up.

"I think you should lie down a little while longer, honey."

"No way!" He shook his head in protest. "My back and that bed aren't the best of friends anyway. I've had enough rest. Came to check on my li'l pumpkin." He smiled at Rosie who was still standing next to him.

"Dad..." Mira started.

He made a face that silently said: *Lighten up! You don't want to worry Rosie.*

Mira got the message.

"Pops, come sit here at the counter with me." Rosie took him by the hand.

"Rosie, Dad's gonna sit at the table today. Why don't you join him there?" Mira interjected.

"I think that's a fabulous idea!" Michael looked at Rosie.

As they headed to the table, Mira could see that her father's health was rapidly declining. He was obviously weak, yet valiantly struggled with each step. She knew he was doing it more for Rosie—than for anyone else and seeing him like that deeply saddened her. More distressing was the fact that there was nothing she could do to change the inevitable.

Rosie sat next to her grandfather, wiggling her feet at the table as she often did.

"Pops, you look really tired. Are you still sleepy?" she asked.

"Just a little tired—yes; sleepy—no," Michael replied.

She continued wiggling her feet, simultaneously staring at him.

"I didn't see you get in yesterday. How was your visit over at the Benjamins' house?"

"It was fun," she answered quickly. "We did sooooo many things, Pops, and Mrs. Benjamin let us help her pick flowers in the garden. They have a huge garden with roses, daffodils and other colorful flowers and Alex got pricked by something and started crying like a baby..."

"Rosie, you weren't teasing, were you?" Sara asked from the stove.

"Pumpkin would never tease," Michael asserted. "She's the most sensitive, loving little girl. I bet you helped make it all better for Alex. Didn't you?"

"How did you know?" She had a bewildered look. "Yes, I made it all better. Mrs. Benjamin was going to take him over to the tap, but I asked her if I could and she let me. Even when he felt sick earlier that day, I helped him feel much better. What I would like to know is why Nana thought that I teased him." She frowned. "My Mom taught me never to tease."

Sara glanced over and realized that she had hurt Rosie's feelings. She turned off the stove and immediately went over to her.

"I'm sorry, pumpkin. I was just playing. I know you're such a good girl." She rubbed her back gently.

"I know, Nana. I wasn't really upset." She smiled.

"Pancakes are ready. Bringing them over now."

"Woo-hoo!" Rosie exclaimed rubbing her hands together. "I absolutely love Nana's pancakes. Don't you, Pops?"

"Yes, I absolutely love them," Michael replied.

Mira took a last sip of her coffee, then got up and joined them at the table. She sat next to her father.

"While Mom's getting the pancakes, could you go and grab my purse, sweetheart? I need to make a dash to the store," Mira said.

"You're going without me?" Rosie asked curiously.

"You actually wanna go?"

"No way, Mom. Pops and I are having pancakes! Tricked ya!" The child merrily skipped off.

Mira leaned in toward her father. "How are you doing, Dad? I mean, how are you really feeling?"

"I feel good." He nodded. "I was a little more tired than usual yesterday. Didn't get much sleep the night before. That's all."

She gazed at him.

"I know all that stuff your mother told you must have caught you off guard, but I'm as strong as an ox. I'll be around for a long time. You'll see. Don't you worry your little head."

Mira's eyes started to well with tears again.

"Now put that away!" He demanded. "We have to think of Rosie. She's too young to handle all the snibbling and snootering and all that crap I don't like."

"Okay, Dad." Mira quickly dried her eyes.

"We'll talk about this some more later, okay?"

"Okay," she replied.

She could see the love in her father's eyes and yearned more than anything right then to find a secluded spot and scream the frustration away. She needed to get it all out. Staying awake for half the night and crying herself to sleep wasn't nearly enough to even begin to ease the pain inside her heart.

Rosie returned a moment later and Sara arrived with the pancakes.

"Thanks, honey." Mira gave Rosie a peck on the forehead for the purse. "I'll see you when I get back."

"Drive safely, now!" Sara said as Mira headed for the door, car-keys dangling in her hand.

* * *

Sara was in the process of clearing the table when there was a knock at the front door.

"I'll get it." She tossed the dish-towel across her shoulder as Michael and Rosie continued their conversation in the dining room.

As was her custom, she never used the peephole, but opened the door right up. She was surprised to see who was standing on her porch. Though they had never met, Sara had a strong inkling as to the woman's identity and the youngster standing beside her.

"I'm so sorry to disturb you," the lady started. "My name is Andrea Benjamin; I live just up the street there. I suppose you're Mira's mother?"

"Oh, yes. And I suppose this handsome young man next to you is Alex?" Sara returned with a smile.

Alex, who had once been staring the older lady down, hung his head shyly when she placed him in the spotlight.

"Rosie hasn't stopped mentioning your name hardly since her first visit. He's such a precious boy," she said to Andrea.

"Thank you. Alex, are you going to say thank you?" Andrea nudged him gently.

"Thank you," the boy answered softly, giving Sara a quick glance before burying his head into his mother's skirt.

"Please come in," Sara moved to the side. "It's nice to finally meet you, Mrs. Benjamin."

Andrea and Alex stepped inside.

"We're not going to take up much of your time, Mrs. Cullen. I was just wondering if Mira was here."

"She went to the store. You can wait if you'd like. She'll be back real soon."

"No, that's okay. You can just let her know that I popped by and I'll speak with her later."

"Well, please let me at least introduce you to my husband," Sara said. "Do come through."

Right then, Rosie appeared. "Hi, Mrs. Benjamin! Hi, Alex!"

"Why hello, Rosie." Andrea smiled. "How are you today?"

"Fine, thank you," the dainty child responded. "Did you come for me?"

Andrea laughed. "I came to see your mom. You know, I promised to take Alex to McKerry's on Saturday. They have the biggest burgers in town. If you want, I can find out from your Mom if you can come along."

"Oh yes! I'd love to come!"

"I'm sure it'll be all right," Sara inserted.

Michael was slowly approaching.

"Honey, this is our neighbor, Mrs. Benjamin and her son, Alex."

"A real, nice pleasure to meet you." Michael extended his hand to Andrea.

"Nice meeting you too, sir," Andrea replied.

"Little man, nice shoes you've got there!" He pointed.

Alex edged in closer to his mother again. "Thank you," he responded almost in a whisper.

"Your husband didn't tag along?" Michael asked.

"No. He's at work, so…"

"I'm terribly sorry we all didn't meet sooner. My sincerest apologies on behalf of my family. Perhaps, we'll meet Mister Benjamin soon."

"Yes. I'm sure," Andrea said.

"Well, I'll be moving along. You all take care now."

"Thank you, sir."

Michael continued toward the master bedroom.

"Are you sure you didn't want to wait for Mira?" Sara asked again. "I have fresh coffee if you'd like a cup."

"That's nice of you to offer, Mrs. Cullen, but I'll have to take a rain-check. Alex and I have quite a number of chores to do. So if you'll just let Mira know I passed by and she can give me a call when she gets the chance..."

"Certainly," Sara walked with them to the door. "I'm glad you stopped by."

"Likewise and good meeting you."

"Bye, Mrs. Benjamin! Bye, Alex!" Rosie cried behind them.

"Bye." Alex waved, happy that he was leaving the house of strangers.

Andrea said farewell to Rosie, then walked with Alex to the car. After hopping inside, she felt an acute sense of relief that Mira actually wasn't there. It was difficult enough forcing herself out in the first place to confront Mira with questions that she wasn't sure she even wanted to ask. She was aware that if Theo knew of her intentions, things would turn out very badly since the unwritten code was that what happened at the house was to remain at the house—no matter what.

She took a deep sigh, started the ignition and drove away.

* * *

"Hey! How are you? I called for you several times." Bobby saw Mira at the check-out line. He was holding a small cart as Mira's items were being struck up at the counter.

"I wasn't feeling so well. Sorry. I told Mom I didn't feel like speaking with anyone," Mira said.

"That's…okay. I totally understand."

"Mom told you?" She paid for the items.

"Told me what?"

"Dad's sick"

The cashier glanced up at them for a moment, then carried on collecting the change from the drawer.

"Really? I'm very sorry to hear that. Hope he feels better soon." Bobby replied.

Mira took the change and grabbed her grocery bag. "I'll wait for you at the door."

Bobby only had two items, so in a minute, he had caught up to Mira and they left the store together.

Several feet away from the entrance, Mira stopped suddenly and looked up at Bobby. "I don't want you to let my dad know I told you this, but he's really sick, Bobby." She felt a lump in her throat and forcefully pushed it back. "Dad has cancer. He's going to die!" Tears started to form again.

Bobby did the only thing he thought to do in that instant. He pulled her close and held her. "I'm sorry, Mira. I'm really sorry." Such news wasn't something he cared to hear about any member of the Cullen family.

The tears were racing down her cheeks now. "I just wanna scream. I need to get this all out," Mira said, her voice breaking.

"Well, why don't you?" Bobby asked. "Don't let anything hold you back."

"You mean…here?"

"Why not? There's a slight chance that someone might call the cops thinking I'm attacking you or

116

something, but you could always explain yourself later if push comes to shove." Bobby thought the remark might make her feel a little better. He couldn't tell if it did.

Without warning, came an ear-piercing scream that had 'eardrum bursting' potential. It may have lasted for thirty seconds.

"That-a-girl," Bobby rubbed Mira's back gently. Her head was resting against his firm chest now.

"Is she all right?" A middle-aged lady stopped and asked.

"She's fine. Just a bit upset," Bobby quickly answered.

"Miss…"

"Yes," Mira raised her head slightly, drying her tears. "I'm fine. Just needed to vent."

The lady gave her a confused look, but took her word for it, nonetheless, and went into the store.

"Feeling better?" Bobby asked Mira.

"Yeah, a little."

"Will you be okay to drive?"

"Yeah. I'm fine now. Thanks."

Bobby walked her to her car.

"So how long does he have?" Bobby asked.

"I don't know. They can't know for sure," Mira responded.

"Well, I'm here for all of you if you need me for anything and I'm still coming by to do the yard work. You'll have to try and convince your dad to leave it to me now."

"I think at this point convincing him to do that might not be so hard."

They were standing at her car.

"I'm sorry I let you down yesterday. Things didn't go as planned."

"I understand, Mira. There's no need to explain. We can do it another time," Bobby returned. "Right now, I know your focus is on your dad and there's no way I'm gonna even try to get in the middle of that."

"Thanks." Mira managed a slight smile. "Just so you know...I've decided to extend my and Rosie's stay for another week or so. Depending on how things progress with Dad, it might be longer. We'll see."

"Okay."

Mira inserted the key into the car door. "I'll see you around, then."

"Yeah. I'll come by the house this Saturday. Remember, when I get there, you have to convince your dad…"

"I know. Thanks for being here for me."

"Don't mention it. Anytime," Bobby replied.

He watched her slowly leave the parking lot and a tear of his own escaped down his cheek as he considered the plight of the man who had become like a father to him—the only one he had ever known.

Mira learned of Andrea Benjamin's visit when she returned home and immediately made the phone call.

"Sure, Rosie can go to McKerry's with you guys," Mira stated. "She'll love it."

"Would you like to join us, Mira?" Andrea asked.

"I would, but Rosie thinks that she and I hang together enough back at home in L.A., so when she comes here, she prefers to do things without me. Strange, but true…"

Andrea giggled softly. "Okay. Alex and I will pop by on Saturday, then. That's also my cupcakes day, so if you want, Rosie can help out and save some for you all."

"I'm sure she'll love to. That's fine, Andrea. And it's so nice of you to allow her to come by so often and play with Alex."

"My pleasure. She's a sweet child."

That was the totality of the conversation as Andrea decided not to veer again into the uncharted territory she had found herself swimming in just hours earlier due to pure and utter desperation.

* * *

That night…

Lights flickered alongside the massive structure, and whispering sounds penetrated the solitude of the child's room. One of the voices was loud and succinct enough in his ear to wake him. Alex peeled his eyes open and as consciousness rushed through his brain, he turned and scanned the bedroom. Only blackness greeted him and silence once again. Then appeared a faint glow near the closet—very small at first, but seemed to be increasing in size and mysterious severity by the second, and forming into something wavy. Suddenly, the indistinct, frenzied whispers started up again—here, there and everywhere. They were coming from all directions, yet the light near the closet remained still, except for its changing shape. In less than a mere minute, it was almost three feet tall. Alex kept looking around as the dread inside mounted to a level by which he could feel his little heart pounding and his throat tightening. It was a truly detestable state as it prevented him from doing the most logical thing—screaming his little lungs out!

The glow was much taller now and taking obvious human form. The outer edges remained faintly light as the inner cavity took on a solid blackness. The thought of what would come was too much for Alex to bear, yet he was helpless, alone, too frightened to make the slightest attempt to run out of there. He squeezed his eyes shut and silently prayed the prayer he had been taught to say every night: 'Now I lay me down to sleep…'

Reluctantly, he opened his eyes again; curiosity had taken hold of him. The shape was still there that was now the height and perfect form of a very tall man—one he had clearly seen wandering through the halls of that very house for months.

Alex yanked the covers over his head and squeezed his eyes shut again. The bold decision lasted only a few seconds as curiosity prevailed a second time and he could not stop himself from peeking. He could see the slight glow through the thin sheets, but to his horror, found that it was now right above him. He shivered with fear beneath the covers, hoping that his parents would somehow know he's in trouble and come to his rescue.

The whispers were louder now: Voices of men and women—young and old. All the while, the unwelcomed silhouette remained stationary, just inches away from him. The boy's breathing became more strained; his chest heaved with fright and at the very moment he felt himself about to black out into utter nothingness, the light disappeared from the sheets and the voices suddenly stopped. Alex shot up out of bed, swung open the door and ran toward his parents' bedroom.

He darted through the open doorway and found his mother sitting up in bed with the lamp on. She had an inexplicable grimace on her face. His father was lying next to her, snoring loudly.

"Baby, what's wrong?" Andrea welcomed her son with open arms as he climbed up next to her.

"He was in my room again, Mama! They were all there!" He sobbed.

"Who was in your room? The shadows?" she probed.

"I heard voices; I think it was them, but I didn't see them this time. He was there too and he was mad."

"Who was, honey?"

"Mister Koney."

The burning on Andrea's back felt most uncomfortable. A fresh one rendered again that night and Theo slept right through her painful shriek. Sometimes, new ones were clawed on top of old ones and the skin of the back was where their focus mainly was. More than ever now, she was convinced the shadow people were set to make her life miserable in that house and possibly drive her out of her mind.

"Who is this Mister Koney?" she questioned the boy.

"You know him, Mama. He's with you everywhere you go, but only in the daytime and only when you're here at home," Alex explained.

An ice-cold shiver went through her. The very thought of what Alex had described was terrifying to the core.

"Are you sure about this, Son?"

"Yes, Mama. I'm sure. He really scares me. He doesn't like me and I don't think he likes you either."

Andrea held him closely.

Just then, Theo rolled over and peeled open an eyelid. "Why is he in here?" he muttered between sleep and wake.

"He's going back to bed now," Andrea said as her husband turned over again—his back facing them.

She looked at Alex. "You know your father wants you to sleep in your own room. How about I stay in there with you again tonight? Would you like that?"

"Yes, Mama," the boy replied.

Andrea slipped out of bed and accompanied Alex to his room. She found that the more she and her son were terrorized by these ghastly forces, the more she was despising her husband and wishing that somehow, these same forces would drag him down to the pit they must have crawled out of.

8

Saturday morning, bright and early, Bobby arrived at the Cullens' house dressed in yard clothes and ready for the weekend routine. Michael and Sara were in their bedroom when they heard the lawnmower going.

"He didn't bother to check with you first as he always does. Wise boy," Sara remarked.

"That's because Mira already laid down the law to me and he obviously knows it." Michael shook his head. "I'll be damned if I'm going to be treated like an invalid around here. I'm going out there!" He put down his mug.

"You're certainly not!" Sara protested. "Unless you're going to say hello to the young man who's out there working for free, you have no reason to go out there right now. There comes a time in life, honey, when we have to allow other people to help us."

"What're you talking about? I always allowed Bobby to help me."

"Yes, you did, but you hardly let him lift a finger." She sighed. "Let him work in peace, Michael. Show him that you don't think you always have to do it yourself in order for it to get done."

Michael looked at her knowing she had won the fight. "All right! I'm going outside."

Michael's movement across the front yard was sort of slow, and Bobby immediately shut off the mower and went over to him.

"Morning, Mister Cullen. How are you this morning?" he asked in his usual upbeat voice.

"Doing good, Son. Thanks for coming by again."

"Don't mention it, sir."

"Guess Mira spoke to you."

"She said you weren't feeling so well and thought it would be best if I just went to work right away instead of disturbing you. Sorry about the noise," Bobby replied.

"I'm A-ok, Son. Nothing serious." Michael thought to convince him. "By the way, the noise sounds good—means the yard is getting done. Will let you handle things today, but I'll be back out here next time right along with you as always, all right?"

Bobby smiled and quickly nodded. "Yes, sir."

Michael watched from the front porch until the sun came out briskly, then he retreated inside the house. Mira and Rosie helped Bobby in the yard until it was time for Rosie to get dressed for her outing.

* * *

Andrea reached for her purse from the couch and tossed the strap across her shoulder. Theo was sitting on the sofa reading the newspaper.

"Tell your Daddy *bye*," she said to Alex who had just trotted down the stairs.

Theo lowered the paper. "Come give Daddy a kiss before you go." He smiled.

The boy hurried over and smooched his father on the cheek.

"Why aren't you coming with us, Daddy?" he asked.

"Daddy's a bit tired today. I'll come next time okay?"

Alex nodded affirmatively.

"We'll be back before four," Andrea told Theo.

"So I don't get a kiss from my wife?" He stood up. Andrea failed to answer, but went over and kissed him. He held her hand.

"I love you, darling. It'll be all right. I promise."

She slipped her hand away from his and headed to the door with Alex.

The child gave his father one last look before they walked out.

12:36pm

The green Buick pulled up in front of the house. Bobby was shirtless and pouring sweat as he raked up the scattered grass leaves into a heap.

"Good day," Andrea hailed as she headed for the front door.

"Hi!" Bobby replied, wiping sweat from his forehead with the back of his hand.

Alex was waiting in the car with the windows rolled down, looking on.

As Andrea approached the door, Mira and Rosie came out to meet her. Sara was standing in the entranceway, waving cheerfully.

The women exchanged pleasantries and Rosie turned back and gave her grandmother a great, big hug. She then hugged Mira.

"I'll see you a bit later, sweetheart," Mira said.

The child skipped toward the car and Alex beamed with excitement that his little friend was joining them.

Sara and Mira stood on the porch as the three drove off into the distance.

"Does she seem all right to you?" Sara wondered.

"Who? Mrs. Benjamin?"

"Uh huh."

"Why do you ask?"

"Looks a little stressed to me," Sara responded.

"The way she looks today was how she looked the first time I saw her," Mira stated.

"I don't suppose it's easy being the wife of a politician."

"I suppose not," Mira agreed. "On another note: That little girl of mine never seems to get enough action."

"And neither did her mother when she was her age." Sara turned to leave.

"Bobby, dear, would you like a cold drink of water?" Sara cried out to him.

"Yes, Ma'am. I could use a little." Mira's eyes met Bobby's. He winked at her and she abruptly followed her mother inside the house.

Mira spent the majority of the afternoon catering to her father's every need. She sort of took over from her mother, wanting to do as much as she possibly could for him. However, the fact of the matter was that Michael did not appear to need much of anything and the constant 'checking up' was beginning to aggravate him. That's when Mira gave it a rest and decided to retreat to her room, if only for a while.

3:13pm

The phone rang and Mira picked up right away.

"We just got back, Mom!" Rosie said happily. She went on and on about the fun they had at McKerry's and how Mrs. Benjamin was getting ready to mix the cupcake batter now.

"That's wonderful, honey. Glad you had such an awesome time. Are you behaving yourself nicely?" Mira asked.

"Yes, Mom. Alex's mom says that I'm a nice, little girl with good manners."

"Yes, you are." Mira smiled.

"How's Pops?"

"He's fine. Watching TV, as usual."

"Well, tell him I'll be back soon and we'll watch TV together for the rest of the night since I had to go out, okay?" Rosie instructed.

"Okay, honey. I'll tell him."

After speaking with her mother, Rosie joined Andrea and Alex in the kitchen. Andrea had the mixing bowl, eggs, flour, sugar and several other ingredients lined off on the kitchen counter. Theo was in the adjacent family room near the back patio watching a ball game on television.

The children thoroughly enjoyed their time helping out in the kitchen and their absolute, favorite part was licking the large spoons and bowl—dirtying their fingers and faces with what remained of the creamy batter. On Andrea's prompting, they soon headed off to the bathroom to wash up while Andrea placed two, long trays of their handiwork into the oven.

"I'll be upstairs getting the toys ready!" Alex exclaimed before racing upstairs. Rosie was still washing her face and hands in the bathroom.

4:25pm

"Mama, where's Rosie?" Alex had dashed downstairs into the living room where his mother was resting.

133

Andrea leaned forward. "I thought she was with you."

"No, Mama. She was in the bathroom washing up and I was waiting for her in my room, but she never came up."

"Did you check the bathroom?"

"She's not there. I looked everywhere and I don't see her," the boy replied.

Andrea immediately got up and went through the house in search of the child, checking every room. Rosie was nowhere to be found. She called out to her repeatedly, but there was no response.

"Where's your Daddy?" she asked Alex, who was trailing behind her.

"I don't know," he answered.

"Theo!" she cried. "Rosie!"

No answer from anyone.

"That's strange. Where could they have gone?" Andrea muttered.

The two went outside to check around the house. Alex instantly spotted a dark shadow figure making its way around the side of the building.

"Mama..."

"What, honey?"

The boy froze and stared at the area in question.

"Someone's back there." He pointed.

Deciding to ensure Alex's safety, Andrea took him back inside, turned off the oven, then returned outside to further investigate. Jogging around to the side of the house, she didn't see anyone, but called out to Theo and Rosie again numerous times. Again—there was no answer.

The yard had a sickening silence around it—one that she had felt inside the house many times, especially at night. There was a light mist in the air as well, which was hugely unusual for that time of day. Then approximately, seventy-five feet near the edge of the property that led into an area of land densely populated by fruit-bearing trees and overgrown brush, she saw Theo advancing.

His white shirt was muddied with dirt and his short, black pants were darted with tiny prickles. He was sweating profusely.

"Where have you been?" Andrea asked curiously. "And where's Rosie?"

The closer he got to her, Andrea could see that the pupils of his eyes had an abnormally darker hue and the expression on his face was blank and unreadable.

"I saw her walk through the family room and out onto the deck," he started. "I thought she was just going to sit outside, but after a while I noticed she never came back in. That's when I went to look for her."

Andrea was listening intently and watching the mannerism that didn't appear to belong to her husband.

"I didn't say anything to you because I thought I'd find her playing in the yard. After I didn't see her, I went further off into the property to look for her, but I have no idea where she went." He shrugged.

"My God! This can't be happening!" Andrea exclaimed, worrying less about Theo's odd behavior and more about the child's sudden disappearance. "We have to find her! How can I possibly look her mother in the face and tell her I don't know where her child is when she was left in our care?"

"We'll find her." He weakly embraced her.

They gave the grounds a thorough search, even wandered some distance out into the forest area with no luck. Andrea slumped down on the front porch with tears in her eyes. "I have to call Mira," she said nervously. "I have to let her know Rosie's missing and we have to call the police."

Theo was sitting next to her. "Call her mother first and let her give the go-ahead to call the police," he suggested.

Andrea got up and went inside the house.

Mira's hair was still damp from the shower when Andrea's call came through. Devastated by the news, she flew to her parents' room, stood in the doorway and said: "Rosie's missing! Andrea said they can't find her anywhere. I'm going down there!"

"Wait for me!" Sara cried.

"I'm going too," Michael started to get up.

Mira stopped suddenly. "No, Dad. You stay here. We'll find her. She just probably wandered off playing somewhere. I'll call you as soon as we find her."

Mira and Sara hurried up the street and Michael walked slowly toward the kitchen door.

"Over my dead body!" he mumbled under his breath.

"What happened?" Sara asked on arriving at the house. Andrea was clearly distraught. She explained everything that happened from the time they got back home from their outing to what Theo had claimed he witnessed while watching television in the family room.

"Did anyone call the police?" Sara pressed.

"I was going to. I thought maybe I'd wait for Mira to get here first," Andrea responded.

At that moment, Mira saw a dark shadow a little ways off into the distance. "Rosie?" she took off into the huge yard. "Rosie, honey!"

Sara and Andrea followed her, but she had them in a fairly wide gap as she attempted to catch up to the

138

figure that moved into the densely-wooded area. Suddenly, another shadowy figure darted in front of her, then another. She stopped in her tracks and looked around at all of them that were assembling in front of her. There were scores of them. The feeling she had at that instant, took her back to the very first day she ever walked onto that property. Fear intermixed with anxiety gripped her as their distinct features gradually came into view.

"Where is my daughter?" she asked. "Where is she?!"

Each of them had an innocence about them that slightly allayed her fear. "The renovations..." Mira said softly.

"What?" Andrea asked behind her.

"The renovations triggered something; brought them back here."

Mira's rambling sounded like gibberish to Andrea and Sara who had no idea what she was talking about.

Then as if on cue, she turned around suddenly and looked toward the old well that still stood near the front of the yard. Sara and Andrea turned too. Rosie, with a frightened look on her face, was standing on top of the old, brick structure as Theo Benjamin stood closely behind her with a crazed glare in his eyes.

"Theo!" Andrea cried. "What on earth are you doing? Get her down from there!"

"Mister Koney..." Alex, who had advanced from the front porch, uttered in a low, but audible voice. He was not referring to his father, but to the ghostly figure that was crouched on top of his father's back.

"Cornelius!" Mira cried in horror as she noticed the exact, same thing. She cautiously advanced toward the well.

"Stay back!" Theo demanded in a loud, raspy voice, clearly not his own. "I had this well built in the year eighteen hundred and fifty-two. Its depth is forty feet into the heart of the ground. When she hits the floor, head first, her neck will crack in half and she will die instantly!"

"Please..." Mira held out her hand. "It's me you want—not her. I was the one who helped Karlen all those years ago. Just let my daughter go!"

As Mira was making her passionate plea to the angry spirit that invaded the soul of Theo Benjamin, Michael drove up into the yard. Shock hit him in the face when he saw Rosie standing at the tip of the empty well. Weak and exhausted, he moved toward the scene as quickly as he possibly could, inhaling deeply and vigorously, for each stride across the lawn commanded it. He knew he had to save her even if it cost him his final breath.

"What're you doing? Get her down from there!" He yelled at Theo; his voice hoarse.

Sara rushed over to Michael and held his arm.

"Pops!" Rosie said meekly with tears streaming down her face.

"You'll be okay, pumpkin. Everything's okay. Just be very still," Michael told her.

"Why are you doing this?" He was a mere six feet away from Theo. "That's my grand-daughter. Please, let me bring her down."

Andrea tried to convince her husband to release the child, but the closer she got to him, the more he inched Rosie closer to the deep, wide hole.

An evil grin escaped Theo's throat as his head spun full circle on the axis of his neck. Mira was grateful for Rosie's sake that the girl's back was facing the horrid sight. If not, fear alone might have murdered her that day.

Mira advanced some more, though cautiously—knowing instinctively that there was no way Cornelius Ferguson would release his grip of Theo who, in a split second, could easily toss the child to her death.

"You don't have to be afraid of him anymore," went a feminine, ethereal voice behind Mira. Glancing back, she saw the shadow figures staring up above them, but for some reason, was not allowed to see what they saw. Nevertheless, she knew who had visited them.

Mira continued toward the well, when suddenly, rushing past her as lightning bolts were the dark shadows that had once stood far behind her. They flew full-force into their former slave-master, bringing him down with a large thump that seemed to shake the earth. Theo, now dazed, stumbled off slightly which caused Rosie to lose balance, and just as she was about to topple into the deep, dark abyss above which she stood,

Michael, who had mustered up every bit of energy inside yanked her from the well in the nick of time. They both fell to the ground—Rosie landing on top of her grandfather.

Mira hugged Rosie tightly as Sara helped Michael up. Andrea ran over to Theo who was still clearly in a daze, having no idea what had just occurred.

Cornelius, trapped beneath the ghosts of his former slaves, emitted blood-curdling screams into the air. Mira and Rosie could hear his painful squeals as those, who once were tortured, ravenously returned the favor. The screams eventually faded into the distance as the otherworldly visitors collectively vanished into thin air.

"Are you all right, sweetheart?" Mira was checking Rosie over.

"Yes, Mommy. Who was that woman in the sky?" Rosie asked.

Mira smiled with a heart full of gratitude—yet again. "Her name's Karlen. She's our guardian angel," she said.

"She's pretty,"

"Yes, she is."

"Why did Mister Koney try to hurt me?" Rosie asked.

"You saw him?" Mira was surprised.

"Yes. Remember I told you from the first time we came here? He seemed so nice at the time."

Mira then realized that Rosie had been seeing the ghost of Cornelius Ferguson from their very first visit there together. She shuddered at the fact that unknowingly, she had been placing her daughter in the presence of infinite evil each time she brought her to this house.

"Yes, honey. I remember," Mira said.

Rosie escaped the grasp of her mother, ran back over to her grandfather and hugged him tightly. "You saved me, Pops. You saved me! I love you soooo much!"

"I love you, too, pumpkin." Michael smiled, though exhaustion fought against the very gesture.

The Benjamins stood together. Theo and Andrea felt terrible about what had happened and Andrea was horrified that her husband could be capable of hurting a child. Mira went over and explained to them what really happened after first explaining the same to her parents, who this time, didn't see any of the ghosts nor understood Theo's actions. Theo was aghast that he could have been used in such a devious way, but Mira tried to explain to him that it wasn't his fault.

"But it is," he answered sadly. "If I wasn't so selfish, but cared more about my family than I did my career and social status, this never would have happened because we would've been out of here a long time ago."

Andrea's heart softened when she heard him say those words.

"I allowed my wife and son to be tortured in this house. What kind of husband and father does that? Could you please tell your daughter that I'm truly, very sorry for what I put her through?"

Mira saw the sincerity in his eyes that were now back to normal. "I will."

Rosie was telling her grandparents where Theo had hidden her before taking her to the well. She revealed how he had tied her to a tree some distance into the wooded area and taped her mouth so that she couldn't scream. More than anything, Michael wanted to walk over there to the fine senator and disfigure his face, but he knew what Mira had told them explained the man's irrational and extreme behavior.

"It was the renovations and the fact that you're a colored family that awakened his ghost," Mira told the Benjamins. "He was brutal in life and no different in death. When you moved in here, the ghosts of some of the former slaves felt the need to protect you—especially your son. Even so, they were still afraid."

"That's why I constantly saw the shadows..." Andrea inserted, "...and Alex did too."

Mira nodded.

"But Alex saw the slave-master as well. He called him Mister Koney, but I never saw him myself."

"Yes, Rosie did too."

"She did?" Andrea was shocked.

"I guess he likes to scare young children," Mira said.

"And attack women," Andrea added.

"Sorry?" Mira wasn't sure what she meant.

Andrea turned around and invited Mira to raise the back of her blouse. On doing so, Mira gasped at the sight in front of her. The cuts closely resembled lashes—similar to what she saw on Andy's back in the vision years earlier.

"*He* did this to you. You know that right? Not the slaves," Mira asserted.

"Cornelius?" Andrea asked.

"Yes."

"What on earth stopped him from harming Alex like this?"

"I suppose the slaves. They may have put most of their energies into somehow protecting him since he was a child and completely helpless."

Theo shook his head in utter amazement. "If anyone had ever told me this story, I never would've believed it. I had to experience this awful thing to be a believer," he said.

Although Mira felt things would be calm now since Cornelius was confronted and overcome by his former slaves, the Benjamins insisted on moving out of the house. Considering he had almost murdered a child, Theo could not have it any other way.

9

Wade and his family showed up for the funeral that was held four months later. It was a rainy day and the Cullen family sat up front under the velvety-green tent at the cemetery. Fortunately, Wade had spent several weeks with his father after the news of his illness and did everything he could to make life more comfortable for him.

Sitting next to her mother, Rosie held a single red rose as tears streamed down her little face. News that her grandfather had died devastated and shocked her as Michael insisted that she not be told of the inevitable before it occurred. He could not bear to see her joy be replaced with weeks or months of sorrow.

Now, as his lifeless body lay before her in the silver casket, the little girl felt the sadness her grandfather wished somehow would never come and the stark reality of a future without him. Wade sat next to Sara and tried his best to comfort her, but he knew that nothing could. The love of their mother's life was gone.

Bobby was in the row behind the family and he, too, was in tears. The Benjamins were also there to pay their final respects. They had long moved out of Cornelius' house, but their newly-formed friendship with the Cullens remained.

* * *

After the death of her father, Mira moved back to Mizpah to be with her mother and enrolled in college to finish her degree. She knew her father would be proud. As for romance, that would have to wait.

Rosie was happy to live in her grandparents' home as every so often, she would have a special visitor—one smiling at her with the love and affection she always felt when he was alive.

About The Author

 Tanya has worn many hats throughout the years as a wife, mother, entrepreneur, and author (just to name a few). She has been writing since she could remember holding a pencil and published her first book titled: 'A Killing Rage' as a young adult. She is now the author of both fiction and non-fiction literature. Most of her books have already made Amazon Kindle's Top 100 Paid Best-sellers' List in several categories. Tanya writes in various genres including: Paranormal Romance, Fantasy, Thrillers, Science fiction, Mystery and Suspense.

Her book *Cornelius*, from which this book is a spin-off, successfully climbed to **#1 in Amazon's Teen & Young-adult Multi-generational Family Fiction** category.

MORE FICTION TITLES BY THIS AUTHOR

Cornelius (Book One in the Cornelius Saga Series)

CARA (Book Three in the Cornelius Saga Series)

We See No Evil (Book Four in the Cornelius Saga Series)

THE CONTRACT: Murder in The Bahamas (Book Five in the Cornelius Saga Series)

The Lost Children of Atlantis (Book Six in the Cornelius Saga Series)

Death of an Angel (Book Seven in the Cornelius Saga Series)

The Groundskeeper (Book Eight in the Cornelius Saga Series)

CARA: The Beginning-MATILDA'S STORY (Book Nine in the Cornelius Saga Series)

The Disappearing House (Book Ten in the Cornelius Saga Series)

Wicked Little Saints (Book Eleven in the Cornelius Saga Series)

Real Illusions I: The Awakening

Real Illusions II: Rebirth

Real Illusions III: Bone of My Bone

Real Illusions IV: War Zone

Immortals Boxed Set Books 1 - 4 (The Entire Real Illusions Series)

INFESTATION: A Small Town Nightmare (The Complete Series)

Haunted Cruise: The Shakedown

The Haunting of MERCI HOSPITAL (Some Patients Never Leave.)

10 Minutes Before Sleeping

Hidden Sins Revealed: The Nick Myers Series, Book One

One Dead Politician: The Nick Myers Series, Book Two

Books Currently in This Series

*Don't miss out on new book releases. Join our
Mailing List Now at: <u>www.tanya-R-taylor.com</u>.*

Made in the USA
Las Vegas, NV
08 March 2022